STEPHEN K. DOMIGAN

◆ EX LIBRIS ◆

Warriors and Maidens

For Steve, our
landscaping warrior!
with all good wishes,

Carolyn Osborn

April 18, 1991

WARRIORS
and
MAIDENS

SHORT STORIES BY
Carolyn Osborn

Afterword by
Marshall Terry

Texas Christian University Press
Fort Worth

Library of Congress Cataloging-in-Publication Data

Osborn, Carolyn, 1934–
    Warriors and maidens / by Carolyn Osborn ; with an afterword by
    Marshall Terry.
            p.   cm.
        ISBN 0-87565-084-8
        I. Title.
PS3565.S348W37   1991   90-49280
813'.54—dc20   CIP

Acknowledgements

"Wildflowers I Have Known" first appeared in *The Paris Review*; "Overlappings," in *New Letters*; "Cowboy Movie," in *The Georgia Review*; "Letter to a Friend Far Away" in *Ascent*; "The Gardener" in *Shenendoah*; "The Greats" in *The Antioch Review*; "The Grands" in *Wind*; and "Songs People Sing When They're Alone," in *American Literary Review*.

The lithograph of the warrior and maiden used on the cover and on the title page is adapted from the original in the Public Archives of Canada, Ottawa, Ontario, C7867.

Design by Whitehead & Whitehead

Contents

For Mary Bess Whidden
and Angela Boone

Warriors and Maidens

Wildflowers I Have Known

*All Texas plants, of course, in the strictest sense are
wildflowers.* . . .
HOWARD S. IRVIN, *Roadside Flowers of Texas*

1. Myself, the Sensitive Briar

ONICA CALLS. There is a confessional tone to her voice and I don't want to hear the confession, the voice, anything. I'm already hung over from the upheavals of the preceding day plus I have a headache from too much dry sherry taken the preceding night. Sherry drinking is preparation for my old age. By the time I'm seventy I'll be able to belt it down with all the other hearty old ladies. I have to be in training for something. Discipline provides a needed order for one who lives alone.

"Craig wouldn't stay on the couch last night."

"I wouldn't expect him to. Craig will never stay on a couch when there's a bed present. Witness mine." At 7:30 A.M. even on the brightest day, it's indecent to discuss a mutual lover yet Monica complains with the best will in the world and I listen with feigned indifference as I'm supposed to be through with Craig. How is anyone ever completely through with anyone? My ex-husband, Dillard, divorced four years ago, calls me from Oklahoma, or Hawaii, or New Brunswick — either New

Jersey or Canada; he makes films and doesn't care where he goes — when he's drunk or feeling lonely he calls and asks if I've quit smoking yet and what's the weather like in Texas. He says he has an abiding interest in bad characters.

Monica carries on. "You've never had three children standing at your door asking for lunch money at 6:30 in the morning. Craig gave it to them."

"That was generous." I try not to sound bitter. Craig never gave me anything but a telephone call. I can't say I love him. I'm sure I don't. So why am I sitting on the other end of a telephone holding my sloppy, envious heart in my hands? I know some of the answers, a survival trick I learned during the years I lived with Dillard: Don't ask yourself questions you don't have partial answers to. Monica now has two men, such as they are, a runaway husband — gone to L.A. with one of his students — and a jelly-like lover who may slip away before she's aware he's gone. Yesterday I had two; George, the over-ardent Arab professor I don't want, and Craig, a would-be husband who asked me to marry him too late. Now I have none. Today all their negative qualities seem less negative, especially after four years of living alone and liking it less. Yesterday I was brave, and free, and strong. Today I'm the dejected reject. Yesterday I laughed at Craig's proposal and sprayed cold water on George and his mariachi band. (Although he's lived in Texas long enough to get a Ph.D., George exists in a state of cultural confusion. He will use any means at hand to court the woman he wants.) Pursuers drive me away, yet once I'm out there running in front of them I begin to feel they have rejected me simply because they can't keep up. I'm playing the game my instincts have been drilled to play for forty years — men hunt, women run — and all the other players have gone. Superior staying power as a long distance runner is no compensation for lovers lost.

I tell Monica as fairly as I can that she'll have to deal with Craig and her children as best she can. It's time for me to go open up my shop. I unchain my bike from the tree on the terrace and am off pedalling furiously up and down Austin's hills, working off all kinds of animosities on the streets.

2. Roselle, Blue-Eyed Grass;
Tom, Red Prickly-Poppy; Mathias, Wild Onion

They're not open yet. I give the code knock and am let in. This is Wildflowers, a florist shop owned by my friend Roselle. She and some other nature lovers run the place. Flower power gone to seed, Roselle says. To look at the exterior you wouldn't think so. Huge galvanized washtubs and buckets are stuffed with fresh flowers. Hanging baskets swing from the wooden awning. Everything smells good: an effusion of brightness and joy spreads over the sidewalk.

Inside it's different. A big live pine Christmas tree Roselle couldn't sell and nobody would undecorate has been standing by the doorway since last Christmas. It is now October. The decorations are eclectic camp — empty pill bottles, a yellow rubber band, white papier-mache pigeons with chicken feather wings, a swag made of interlocked pop-top rings, a lost key, one ordinary shiny red ball that assumes sexual significance hung next to a clear plastic icicle.

Farther in the interior there's a chopping block, a tree stump where long-stemmed flowers are relentlessly sliced off, and a dusty old wicker baby buggy filled with baby's breath, a depressing object I think. Roselle loves it. Behind the buggy is a piano that someone, name unknown, comes in to play when he feels like playing. Someone is tall, has dark curly hair, plays only classical, and is rumored to be a rich man's son. The unknowns in Roselle's life are usually mysteriously rich until proven poor. This may never happen. There's very little attempt to prove or to explain anything at Wildflowers. People wash in and out, objects collect.

Roselle and Tom, her main helper and current live-in

3

lover, are sitting on the edge of an ancient moldy pink couch twisting wire around small bouquets of black and white roses.

"Somebody giving a *danse macabre?*" My early morning rancor, stifled until now by play-acting with Monica, seeps out.

"Integrated wedding," Tom snaps back. A self-made Marxist, he's brisk, efficient, all common sense, no nonsense. Roselle surrounds herself with a mixture, half-and-half, of people like Tom and those like her, vague, indecisive, kinky. She floats back and forth between the two worlds, one foot suspended above the wild side, one above the tame.

"Why don't you spray everything gray?"

Roselle looks up and grins. "It's not an integrated wedding, just a couple of freaks getting married." Except for her uniform, jeans and the first shirt she lays hands on in the morning, she resembles the illustrations of princesses in the *My Bookhouse* volumes I read as a child. If George, the Arab, with his indiscriminate passion for blue-eyed blondes ever saw us together, he'd suffer harem visions. I'm the leggy sort. My hair is short and honey-colored, my eyes are dark blue. Roselle is smaller, younger, in her late twenties; she has long straw-colored hair and light blue eyes. Jailed once for possession of pot, she's on probation now and has given up growing marijuana in her greenhouse.

Handing Tom a dripping bunch of daisies so he can whack the long stems off, I wander into the greenhouse. One room, skylighted, it stands thin wall to thin wall next to Andrew's Barbershop. For all her dedication to the beauties of the earth, Roselle lacks the right touch with green plants. She does well raising all-flowering types and can make the surliest camelia bloom, but she either tries too hard or cannot truly love philodendron, dieffenbachia, or any other common green leaf. I'm looking at a brown-edged Boston fern when through the wall I hear a customer at Andrew's saying, "What this town needs is a good whorehouse."

Lots of discussions about what this town needs go on at Andrew's. He satisfies one of those needs, a barbershop where

4

a man can still get a haircut for eight dollars — the reason he's open now. If you make a living doing eight-dollar haircuts, you have to be up early. "Most people don't realize they need a haircut till they look at themselves hard in the mirror first thing in the morning. That's the moment of truth," Andrew has told me. He's Chicano, but has adopted an English name; Andres anglicized to Andrew sounds more American. Since they're both minorities, he and the Wildflowers get along well. Some of his customers don't understand this; most of them never know it. While sitting in the barber's chair they make elaborate plans for Andrew to cut off long hair or, if possible, shave it off — another thing this town needs, less longhairs. They curse "hippies" vehemently. A disparaging category is a long time dying in the West. Andrew pays no attention, lets them vent their wrath, and for Christmas gives Roselle a calendar full of colored pictures of saints.

When I go back to get my daisies I see Mathias has burst in. I didn't hear him, yet I'm sure he exploded in the doorway in a huff. He's one of the wilder ones, forever in trouble or just about to be in trouble.

"The guy across the street says we took his bear!"

"Oh God! Who wants it?" Roselle asks.

Hal, the guy across the street, is a filling-station owner, and his bear is a big stuffed brown one he shot on the only trip he made to Alaska. Generally it stays in an unused carwash stall, looking sadly through dirty glass panes. My crafts shop is right next to the stall so I pass the bear every day. I'll miss him. Some people have familiar statues they pass in parks. I had the bear. Glass-eyed though he was, he seemed to contemplate the daily scene with equanimity, and why shouldn't he? He was stuffed, forever rearing on his hind-paws, in an attitude of aggression. Fearsome, all threat and no bite, unable to scratch his own fleas, and what is more, unable to feel them, all hostility safely expressed in his stance.

Mathias stumbles around flailing his arms, his hair zinging out in all directions, a new-made scarecrow scared.

5

Roselle is snipping off pieces of wire to twist around the last black and white bouquets. "We get blamed for everything. Who would take a stuffed bear? Why should I — "

"Mathias?" Tom has one of the virtues of the simplistic thinker — he doesn't mind jumping to obvious conclusions.

"It was on a stand with little wheels. The door wasn't locked." Mathias grins so self-confidently that I'm now sure of his intentions. The eternal prankster who takes only apparently useless things — he's made off with Roselle's empty milk cartons, a whole side of a barn that collapsed (he gave that to Roselle who used it for panelling the inside of the shop), a cardboard box of notes for somebody's dissertation, a hideously painted ceramic Sleepy dwarf from an over-decorated lawn — he says he's just cleaning up trash. I've gone along with him till this moment, especially as he's never graduated to professional burglary. Now I see it is his pleasure to steal and to boast about the theft. Since he's stolen a figure from my landscape, I'm as angry as any outraged citizen missing a bronze Robert E. Lee.

"You should have seen me at three this morning pushing him along the sidewalk."

"Where is it now?" I ask.

"In cold storage. Best place for a bear from Alaska."

"Here?" Menace edges Tom's voice. He is tall and physically well-filled out. Mathias, just as tall, is skinny and flushed with frantic pride.

"Didn't you see him when you got the roses?"

"No, we were in a hurry."

"Must have been the sheet — camouflage."

We all go into the cold storage room behind the couch. There, next to the wall behind two buckets of pink carnations, a bulky white shape looms, paws showing a little underneath the sheet. There's something pathetic about those exposed claws — somehow they remind me of all the nights I've spent in bed alone trying to warm my own cold feet.

6

"Really d-u-m-b." Tom spells out certain words. "You know the cops will look here. Where did you plan to put him after he cooled off, Mathias?"

"I didn't — I mean I didn't have any long range — Uh . . . I . . . I don't know."

Tom's attention jumps to the immediate problem. "Let's see — We could put him in the delivery truck, keep the sheet, flowers on the sides, cover him with palm fronds and take him — " He looks at me.

"Oh no! My apartment isn't going to be hideout for Mathias' bear."

"Just today. Then we'll find another place."

"No."

"I'm freezing," Roselle says in a dreamy soft voice. We all move out of cold storage. "We could ask Andrew."

"No time. He's too close. They're bound to look there. This wedding is at eleven and we're not even through with the flowers for it."

"Please," Roselle implores me. Usually I'm an easy touch, too willing to help anyone in need. Today the continual answer is, "No!"

"You'd never get him down the stairs to my place. He's too heavy to carry."

"Naw. He's light. Hollow inside. Two of us could carry him." Mathias, the lifter stating his professional opinion, looks pleased.

"How are you going to disguise him? My landlady is around all morning and so are the other tenants. Herr Strook has nothing else to do but watch people coming in or going out. He'll tell Mrs. Gaither he's seen you and the two of them, together with their gothic imaginations, will decide you're delivering a corpse."

Tom squats down in front of me. "Just for today, Margaret. We'll tell your landlady it's a piece of furniture . . . an antique couch with claw feet."

7

Roselle giggles.

"She won't believe it. The place is crammed with furniture already."

"Margaret, you've got to help us. If I get caught doing anything the slightest bit illegal, I'll get sent back to jail." Every time Roselle mentions jail she shudders, and I shudder for her.

"What about my shop?" I ask.

"Too close."

"What about — ? Hapsell, yes. Maybe he will."

"Who's Hapsell?"

"Sculptor. Lives above me and Herr Strook. I'll call him." How can I phone Hapsell and ask him to take in a cold/hot bear? How can anyone ask favors? Do unto others as you have done for them. I've done plenty for Hapsell including sheltering his girl when his rich aunt came for a two-week visit, and taking him homemade soup when he was stricken with flu. I call. He agrees to hide the bear if Tom promises to move it tomorrow. One more thing in his studio won't bother him for a day.

3. Pop Sigh, the Great Pokeweed

I wheel my bicycle in, take the CLOSED sign off the door of my shop, put the daisies in a vase, sit down on a stool behind the counter, and hope no one comes in for thirty minutes at least. The thing to do is to stay in bed. Stay in your own room. Don't go out. It's not safe on the streets. You can get mugged, kidnapped, raped, run over, lose your lover, be opportuned by friends. It's nothing, I tell myself: people go through these phases. You can be living a quiet reasonably content life, then the moon changes, events pile up, accidents happen. I was all right before, wasn't I? There was the shop, my customers, my scattered friends, a drink at five with Hapsell when he was between girls, a little light-minded philosophy about the acceptance of things as they are, laughter

8

over mundane foibles. Now I'm feeling desperate and trapped. How did I get here? Huddled on top of a high stool, feeling the invisible yet heavy weight of a dunce's cap, I wonder: By what crooked route did I arrive?

Is my background important, my family the key? No amount of speculation will change it. I can wander through ancestral halls shouting for everyone to come out and be accounted for and who'll turn up? Ghosts of good burghers muttering about being disturbed, one or two zanies who evidently passed on their proclivities to me, one known drunk (how many unknown?), an uncle of generations past who found the New World so disappointing he returned to Ireland in time to be one of the potato famine's victims, women who raised families and went to church on Sundays, an aunt who painted weak yellowy, greeny, pinky landscapes.

I have the regulation number of parents; a married sister, Cicily, living in London; a brother, Jack, who's a marine biologist working on the Texas coast. I don't see him often. How I arrived here has little to do with them. I didn't choose to be the oldest. If order of birth has anything to do with who one is, and I grant it generally does, I have played the elder child. Used to sit up nights with my parents wondering what to do about Jack, the youngest, if he ever did come home. I didn't take piano lessons because Cicily, the middle one, needed something only she could do. Nor can I say I missed those lessons. Painting, though I had no true talent, was left to me as science was left to Jack. You would have thought my parents were trying to provide the faculty for a small liberal arts college. They did the best they could with the material on hand. It's not their fault I would not persevere. Somewhere along the way Jack and I switched places; I became uncertain about exactly what my life would be and he became the eldest, responsible, settled, producer of grandchildren. He reads the newspaper every morning. I catch the headlines out of the corner of my eye while passing the newsstand or wait till Hapsell or Herr Strook or Roselle tell me the news. Years ago, a stranger stopped me on the street and told me when Nixon resigned. People will act as couriers. Town criers cry on any street. Everyday I mumble the escapist's prayer, "Oh Lord, keep the real world away from me!" while Jack, gnashing his teeth through his morning bowl of granola, hollers, "Bring it on!" I don't know what Cicily says. The last time I talked to her she'd adopted an English accent. By the time that much nasality has frosted over a Texas drawl and is pushed through a trans-Atlantic cable at 5 A.M., you can't hear much more than, "Ahlo, love!" and "Ta-ta, deah!" — one of the shorter summations of life.

From hello to goodbye there is the space between, and whatever mixture of heredity, environment, and bad luck led me here, here be I. Were my parents feeling anxious at the moment I was conceived? In Adam's fall did we sin all? What is the First Cause? Why do children turn out like they do? Shall I call my friendly hometown geneticist and ask him? Am I a combination of my father's benign cynicism and my mother's gleeful softness? Was it raining the day I was born? Can blame be laid? I would like to lay some. Shall I record my dreams and thereby reveal all terrors and fearful wishes? Pop Sigh, please take note:

"I'm on an elevator that goes awry. Instead of going up and down it careens sideways spiraling around the interior of a building, usually a hotel. I'm trying to get to a particular room in order to meet someone and I can never make it."

"Ah, my dear. The hotel, a tall building, yes? A place where people sleep. A phallus. You desire to meet someone who will give you the orgasm. You can never make it. You wish to be made . . . laid, yes?"

"Yah! Yah! But, I ask you, is this the key to my soul?"

"Nein . . . to the libido."

Oh, I love Pop Sigh. Crazy about him. He arranges my confusion in labelled groups. In order to please him I invent dreams such as the one above. Notice how well he handles American slang, this wise old man whose presence I invoke whenever I'm in need of a companion. Usually I put him in a convenient corner. He smokes a cigar and, like Einstein, wears white socks.

"Pop, I've drifted to the backwater of existence. I'm here in the brackish atmosphere of my shop surrounded by dried flowers, needlepoint kits, unpainted wooden boxes, shells, African trade beads, quilt-frames, lumps of clay in five- and ten-pound bags, papers of all colors and sizes, all things ready to be made. My last known lover is making my best friend. I know. Monica called and complained to me this morning. What am I to do?"

"Wait." Pop flicks his cigar ash on the floor and is gone. Sometimes he moves by his own volition. I am not totally in control. I hate waiting. Patience, like most virtues, is monotonous.

4. Bullnettle

Heavens, what a handsome young man! Haven't I seen him somewhere before? But you don't say, "Haven't I seen you somewhere before?" to a policeman. I walk half-way across the room to meet him.

"Can I help you?"

"I'm looking for a stuffed animal. He's got dark curly hair."

"I can't help you much there. People usually make their own. I don't know of a crafts shop that carries forms . . . no plain white unbleached muslin animals waiting to be decorated if that's what you've got in mind. I can supply buttons for eyes, or bells for buttons, or — "

"I don't want to make a stuffed animal."

He appears to agonize as I say, "Well, it's all right if you should want to. A lot of men have taken up crafts lately. I've got three male customers who embroider, not to mention the knitters and the rug makers."

"No!" His hands make a definite negative movement in the

air before him, the fingers tensed and strong. I know now where I've seen him.

"Are you a pianist daylighting as a policeman or a policeman moonlighting as a pianist?"

"Neither one. Both."

"I thought so."

He groans. "Do you know where they've put that bear?"

"Who is 'they'?"

"The Wildflowers. I don't know what to do. If I went to Andrew's to look they would hear every word. How can I arrest Roselle when I've been using her piano free for six months? You don't find that many old Steinways laying around for free practice, and it's in perfect tune."

"Could you take off that uniform? It's a lovely color of blue, but I can't talk to you when you're in uniform. It's a block I have."

"You want me to strip here at 9:30 A.M. in the middle of a crafts shop?" He begins fumbling with his tie knot.

Andrew walks in and asks if I've got change for a twenty. He looks at the piano player/policeman, winks at me, and goes to the cash register. I give him change and nod toward the storage room. He grins, then follows me. Andrew loves intrigue. I let him out the back door.

The policeman is brooding over jars full of marbles. "I can't take my clothes off in front of a strange woman."

"I'd like to know why not? Women strip their clothes off in front of thousands of strange men every day. Maybe you need background music. Let's see — No, I guess we can't go over to Roselle's and let you play."

"Play the piano and strip at the same time! That's physically impossible. What if I just took off my badge?"

I shake my head.

"How do I know you really know anything about that bear?"

"You don't, but I do."

"I believe you are enjoying this."

"I am. I also intend to do something about it. Andrew has gone to get one of those striped smocks he throws over his customers. I hope you'll throw it over your threatening blue shirt."

"Are you going to have him cut my hair too?"

"No. I try not to carry things too far."

5. Goat's-Rue

I do though, I get carried by events, people, my own emotional acrobatics. I begin a day crawling off misery's floor, end it after midnight doing a highwire act consisting of Mathias, Tom, me, and the bear. We wouldn't let Roselle help because of her police record. Jack, the pianist/policeman, would lose his job if he were caught. Andrew was peripheral and didn't need to be dragged in. Hapsell's help extended to lifting the bear into the van. Beyond that he wasn't necessary. Neither was I until I convinced Tom a look-out was essential.

Taking a bear is one act; taking it back is another. We try to impress this on Mathias who is downcast about the whole enterprise. He seems to think the job is too easy.

"Nothing to it. You flip the door open and push him in."

"How much noise does the door make?" Tom asks. Oh, there should be a Tom in every group, someone who foresees danger in the mundane, someone who knows a rattling door can draw an enraged gun-toting-Alaskan-bear-hunter-filling-station-operator out of the bushes growing beside his carwash stall.

Which is, of course, what happens. Almost forty years of living amidst gun-toters had not prepared me for the fear that ripples bones when gaping at the end of a shotgun. Two small round circles, a beast with eyes set too close together. I choose the idiot's method of confrontation, looking at something else. My eyes swerve to the gun-holder's shoes. They are crepe-soled. I can't see what color. At once I decide: I will not be shot by a man wearing crepe-soled no-colored shoes.

"Put that down!" Being scared doesn't wash out indignation.

"You all stole my bear!"

He continues holding the gun on me. Mathias and Tom have already gotten the bear back in place and are crouching behind it. I stand by the open door wondering why I had been so determined to see Mathias return something he'd stolen.

"We all didn't. If you don't put the gun down I'm not going to talk to you anymore." I start walking away relying on the code which doesn't allow shooting in the back, especially not women.

"How come you're here putting him back in the middle of the night if you didn't take him in the first place? Say, aren't you the girl from next door?"

We progressed to the corner street light which gave Tom and Mathias room to run to the van. "Have you put that gun down?"

"Yeah."

I turn around. "My name is Margaret. I own the crafts shop. You're Hal, aren't you?" He didn't seem so angry now. "Is that the gun you killed the bear with?" It isn't, but he needs some more cooling down time.

"No'm. This here's a twenty-gauge, a bird-hunting gun. Now for a bear, you need a magnum."

I watch the traffic light change, cars whizz by. Across the street, music pours out of a bar. What am I doing here in the middle of a medium-sized city, talking to Hal, a gas jockey who is convinced he's a great hunter? Dan'l Boone kilt Bar. He carved that message on a tree years ago and years haven't done away with Dan'l. He stalks city streets right now.

"How'd you get him?" Who cares? Nobody but the victim, the hunter, and other hunters who'll listen to a "How I Got It" tale knowing that's the price for getting to tell their own. Hal has been too busy at the gas pumps for too long, or maybe all the hunters he knows have forsaken him. As it happened, he'd gone to Alaska to rope a bear.

"Why?" We are sitting on a wooden bench by the front door of the station; cars thin out a little as we talk. I'm not sure where Tom and Mathias have gone. The van is still there.

"I used to rodeo a lot. I was a roper. You know what I mean?"

I nod. In the little Central Texas town where I grew up there was a rodeo every summer.

"There was this fellow, Dillard Williams, here in town wanted to make a movie of me roping a bear. I didn't have nothing much else to do. It was before I started running this station, and the rodeos round here was over, and I was broke. He flew me up to Alaska. We had to look a long time, had to get a guide even. I didn't have no horse. Wouldn't have helped none, bear's too heavy for a horse, but if you're a roper you get used to working with a horse. You know what I mean?"

I said I did. Not in the way he meant though. Being married to Dillard about ten years I knew more, and less, than I thought I should. All that time he was in Alaska he told me he was shooting a wildlife documentary. He didn't say anything about concocting a rodeo extravaganza.

"A horse would've shied anyway." Hal was genuinely grieved about not having that horse. "We tried to find a bear near some trees so I could tie him. I wasn't going to tie him long, just long enough to get the pictures made. So there was me, and the guide, and Dillard taking pictures when we found the bear. I roped him okay, but he didn't pull against the rope like a calf does. He came toward us while I was getting the rope to a tree. Mad! Lord, lady, that bear was mad, on his hind legs running at me. I couldn't drop the rope. It was like I was stuck to it. If you been roping all your life you don't let go easy. Besides, Dillard was shouting, 'Great action, great! Hold him, Hal! Hold him!' So I was trying to run backwards and I fell. The guide shot the bear. He fell on top of me. I nearly died of suffocation. I never been so . . . so mortified, getting my picture took with a bear on top of me. The guide thought we was plain fools. He cussed me and Dillard half a day, and we was in bad trouble. My leg was broke, and the bear was shot out of season. But Dillard — He's so rich he don't have good sense. He told the guide he'd pay the fine. We went on back to Juneau, sent another plane with the guide to get the bear. Dillard had him skinned out, and stuffed, and gave him to me. We been together since. I don't rope no more."

Hal stared at the driveway through the station, and I stared too, remembering Dillard's get-rich-any-minute-now fantasies. The year of the bear-roping movie was probably the one I learned a good soup could be made from chicken necks.

"Listen, Hal, I like your bear. I say hello to him every morning when I come to work. I didn't take him. I only helped bring him back. The guy who took him is a kind of nut, I guess."

"Like me and Dillard." Hal grinned.

"No. You and Dillard have more imagination. Thank you for telling me about the bear." I get up, stretch, and walk away, leaving him sitting there on the bench fondling his shotgun. I find Tom and Mathias both huddled in the back of the van. All the way to Roselle's Tom and I cuss Mathias. Among other things I call him, "A wrong-headed four-toed pissant," and Tom follows with "Babbling bourgeois bum."

Mathias doesn't look contrite; he looks interested, as if he's wondering what we'll think to call him next. He'll take any kind of attention he can get. I poke Tom with my elbow and we both shut up. Sighing to ourselves and grinding our teeth, we make the common noises of nightmare dreamers hopelessly awake.

6. Cocklebur

When I get home I give Hapsell his van key and start down to my apartment. Herr Strook is still up, determined not to miss anything tonight, I guess. He stops me outside his door.

"Margaret, have you been decorating your terrace?" He's peering over my left shoulder so I turn and look. There, by the glow of the porch light I've left on for myself, I can see someone has scribbled something with green chalk all over the cement.

"No. I haven't been — kids maybe?"

"My dear friend, there are no children in this neighborhood." He bends over the railing beside me. "I believe it is a message of some sort. The script is difficult though."

I push past him to run down the stairs. George, the ardent Arab, has snuck back in the night and written something in Arabic on the square of cement in front of my door. A note flutters from the doorknob. "I have written this poem for you. Love, George."

It's probably wretched sentimental poetry about his heart and mine entwined beneath moon-drenched date palms silhouetted against midnight-blue skies. I stare at the green loops and whorls feeling dizzy, then I hear a voice from above.

"You want me to translate for you?"

I look up. In the fork of the oak tree, like a genie who has popped out of a bottle, is George.

"No. I'd rather look at the design."

"Margaret, you are difficult."

There is some truth in this. However, loss of a would-be husband through bad timing is no reason for being won by a man who has nothing to recommend him but persistence.

"Try not to be so difficult to woo."

He sounds regrettably like an owl. His feet — he's wearing sandals as usual — have a fascinating resemblance to owl claws curled around the limb. I fumble in my pocket for the key. Once it's in the door, I look up again at George who's still perched in the tree.

"I can't have you sitting around in my tree all night, George. I'm going in. You must go home."

"I will not. I will sleep in front of your door."

"That will be uncomfortable."

"Margaret, are you speaking to me? I can't hear you," Herr Strook calls.

"Who is that?" George quavers.

A voice in the night may be any voice. "My father. He's just arrived and is upstairs saying hello to Hapsell." I pause to let the information take effect.

"Yes, I'm going in," I shout to Herr Strook. To my left I hear George scrambling out of the tree. Amazing. Even the imitation father of a middle-aged woman can send an over-ardent Arab home. I slam the door behind me hoping a rain will wash away George's green chalk. If you lose control of events, you can always hope natural forces will intervene on your side.

Chauffeur

LASS CURTAINS covered the window like an almost impenetrable mist, a breath winter had left on the glass, yet she could see the old white Cadillac moving slowly up the street that led to the capitol. Filmore was back. An odd, inexplicable part of her life, Amy hoped he wouldn't stop by the office soon. She was busy and Filmore required time. He'd come by eventually, judging from his actions in the past. For some reason, he wouldn't come to her house. Apparently he'd connected her in his mind to business, so he saw her only at her law office though she'd never done any legal work for him nor for anyone he knew. She imagined he simply showed up there because he found her there. He wouldn't have thought to look up A. Wilson's home address in the black and white pages of the Austin directory; instead he remembered she was a lawyer. Probably he hadn't known many women lawyers.

She turned her eyes back to the papers on her desk thinking about Filmore's refusal to look for her at home. Where was his home now? Did he have a family or live by himself? And if he was by himself, how did he take care of the demands of everyday life? It was hard to imagine him doing a washing, reds running into whites, water running down his arms, or cooking — dicing, chopping, his long fingers clearing onions off a cutting board. Oh, no. He could do neither. He was so closely connected, in her memory, with luxury, with lying. She'd met him a long time ago in New Orleans, four years ago, wasn't it? Her dissolute period when she'd first gotten divorced and run back home to visit her parents. Now she lived in a house alone, a small one bought at an outrageous price in Clarksville, an expensive area close to town, and she'd spent more than she should have restoring it. Once a neighborhood filled with freed slaves and later occupied by their descendents, Clarksville remained stubbornly integrated though white dollars flooding in threatened to wash away that pattern.

Amy was pleased with the present mixture; it was an ideal that would take other parts of Austin years to accomplish. Sometimes she wondered if real integration would ever happen. Even this far west, customs changed slowly. Born in the South, the whole struggle was so deeply a part of her life, she almost forgot it at intervals. Some days she felt she lived in Clarksville simply because it was pleasant to be able to walk to work.

A small Victorian house built about 1886 near the capitol served as her office. Her house was built in 1906. She found both satisfying. Brought up in New Orleans, she'd learned to like old things about her, though she still liked younger people and contemporary art. She smiled at her foolishness even as she wondered if, like many older women, she'd some day prefer younger men. That answer was to come, wasn't it? Divorced at thirty-five, now forty-one, she would have to watch her predilections. She worked out other people's problems well — she'd made her reputation in divorce law — but she was often terrible at solving her own. Filmore was the strangest one she had at the moment.

When she first saw him in Austin last year about the same time, she'd hardly known him. Her secretary Marialice had shown him into the office. He'd sat down in front of the desk, his cap perched on his knees, one hand running over the taut black material on top. Was he one of the clients' driver? She couldn't remember a client rich enough to afford a chauffeur. Was he, perhaps, a client himself?

"Yes?" Her chair creaked a bit as she leaned toward him. He was an elegant looking black man, tall, thin, immaculate. His uniform was well-tailored. How old was he? Old. She could never tell exactly. And she couldn't think of a black chauffeur she'd ever known except . . . except. . . . Leaning back in the stiff leather chair, she felt time lurch, drunkenly reel away. There was something, something she didn't — She stared at him wordlessly while he continued to caress his hat.

"I'm sorry. I . . . I. . . ." She stood up and offered her hand, and as she looked into his eyes, reddened by fatigue, she decided quickly because she remembered he didn't drink, she knew who he was.

"Filmore. Aren't you Filmore, Mr. Roden's chauffeur?"

The old man stood before her, holding his hat as if it was some sort of talisman, and bowed his head. "I thought . . . I thought I would find you somewhere and you would know me, Mrs. Amy."

He eased himself back into the chair. "It took me a long time . . . long, long time. If you be married, I knew it would take forever. But you're not. I found you in the yellow-page directory. Looked for you every town in Texas I went through."

She thought she saw him smile but couldn't be sure. His pleasure at being recognized was evident in his tone of voice. "No, I haven't married again. I might someday."

"Mr. Roden — He don't like that."

"Filmore — " She paused for a moment wondering if he had accepted Arthur Roden's death. He'd had time enough to. "Filmore, you know . . . you know he's gone."

"Umm. Left me this car . . . this Caddy. His last." Arthur had died three years ago in New Orleans, one of his favorite places. Somebody, an ex-wife most likely, had arranged a jazz funeral for him. "Just A Closer Walk with Thee" marched everybody slowly to the graveyard; "The Saints," that joyful song, danced everybody back. Amy hadn't gone. She hadn't known he was dead until an old friend in New Orleans called to tell her. She wouldn't have gone to his funeral if she had known. Arthur was married when she met him.

She had loved him in a shameless, hopeless way. It wasn't anything she could do anything about. Some passions were like diseases, like catching the flu. Feverish, aching, just divorced, she endured. It was all wrong, and the timing proved to be the worst part. He was married to Rosalie Evans, his third wife and a friend of hers. To complicate matters further, Arthur, twenty years older, always fell in love with younger women, so she eventually learned she wasn't special; she was only that season's necessity. At the time, however, the evident difference in their ages seemed merely classic and rather comic, ridiculous almost as the sight of their bodies in bed might have been to any of those benign and randy Greek gods.

"Filmore — "

He had drifted to the window where he seemed to be staring at the car. That was his special quality, to disappear when people wanted to be alone.

"Did Mr. Roden's third wife — ?"

"They divorce. After he and you part. Mrs. Three divorce him quick. He die in New Orleans by himself. Except for me."

"But who took care of the funeral?"

"Mrs. Three, Mrs. Rosalie. She still live there then. She gone now."

"Well — ?"

"I drive myself from Lousiana back to Tennessee, to Foxton, to look at it again. It's a golf club now." He moved slowly back to the chair.

"I know. I'm sorry."

"Lots of grown men running round with those little sticks

and balls out where Mr. Arthur's mamma had her vegetable gardens. They kept the rose garden, some of it."

She listened closely as he told the familiar story, heard his quavering, grinding voice as he spoke of the injustice of change and the bitterness of loss, of the displacement of everything he'd known by trash and trivia. Beneath his mournful recitation ran time's river sighing gone, gone, gone. And there was no giving it back. Foxton had been Arthur's father's estate. Arthur was not sentimental about property. He sold it to the golf club just as he might have sold it for a cemetery site, an orphan's home, or a college campus. He had other houses.

He'd told her, "There's a time to sell, Amy, and a time to buy."

"You sound like Ecclesiastes."

"Can't help it, honey. It's the truth. I mean to sell Foxton soon as I can. And you know who is most upset about it, my chauffeur! God-amighty!"

His curse was a groan, a brief weakness breathed away and scarcely noticeable, the only unemphatic part of Arthur. He was determined about everything else.

"Well, of course, he has some feelings about the place. He was your daddy's last chauffeur, didn't you tell me?"

"Ahh! Next thing you'll say is Filmore and I are more kin than I know."

"No. . . . I never — "

"Might as well as. Only I know we're not. Daddy didn't have any of those leanings, didn't lust after chocolate."

"I don't know how you'd know that."

"I do though. Filmore's like him in one way. He's a conservative. Gets used to things. Likes them to stay as they are. It has upset him considerably whenever I've divorced."

He leaned back and laughed so heartily she began to dislike him. His laughter provided a space between them, the first thin line of objectivity which would, in time, widen. He couldn't imagine his chauffeur or anyone else attached to him,

23

no matter how loosely, might have a life totally apart from his. He couldn't imagine her taking a deposition, or counselling a client, or even questioning a witness in the courtroom. Why should she do those things when he needed her? Anyone around Arthur reflected his needs in some fashion. He wanted somebody to be upset when he divorced, when he sold his father's estate, when he wrecked the Cadillac so badly he had to buy a new one. Filmore mourned every time.

* * *

The first visit he made she said, "You can't just go roaming around Texas and Louisiana and Tennessee, Filmore."

"Didn't you, Mrs. Amy?"

"Not really. I was back home visiting when I . . . when I met Mr. Roden. Aren't you tired of traveling?"

"Yes'm."

"Why don't you settle somewhere?"

"Folks mostly gone now."

She thought of telling him her own family was gone also but that seemed too much like something Arthur would have said. In essence his advice was: Be like me and you'll be all right.

"I don't like to bother you — "

"You're not bothering me." Of course she had calls she should answer, people coming in. They would have to wait.

"Could I take you for a drive, just a short one? I already know this town. We go up by the capitol and down the avenue, then I'll loop back."

Amy watched him turning his cap round and round with both hands. Did he simply want a passenger? That couldn't be. Maybe he wanted somebody he knew, somebody who'd known Arthur.

"All right," she said slowly. "All right. I'll make a trade with you. You take me for a drive and I'll take you to lunch."

She used to wonder where he ate when he delivered them to yet another one of Arthur's awful little holes. Like a lot of southern men, he liked Cajun and corn pone cooking. In New Orleans, in the midst of one of the few collections of real

24

chefs in America, Arthur sought out red beans and rice. What did that leave for Filmore? Did he go to a soul food place on down the street? Sometimes she thought he might be in one of the better French restaurants eating sole bonne femme while she and Arthur were mushing through yet another bowl of gumbo.

"I don't think we can, Miss Amy." He shook his head, his face wrinkled into a disbelieving frown.

"It's all right, Filmore. Black people and white people get along well here."

"I don't know. I know the streets some. That's all. I can't say that I know how these people be."

She left the office with him giving Marialice a slight wave as they went out. The car was so exactly the same she stopped to gaze at it a moment. Arthur had not been particularly fond of cars. He wanted something dependable, comfortable, and classic. No, he would not have a foreign car. Old wartime animosities against the Germans rose and conquered his desire for a Mercedes. He would have, finally, what his father had, a Cadillac, white to reflect the sun, always white so he wouldn't have to make up his mind about color. White outside and in. The seats were white leather.

Filmore opened the back door.

"Thank you, no. I think I'll ride up front." Sometimes when Arthur came to get her he'd be sitting there with his chauffeur.

"No!"

His voice was so sharp, his circumspect manner so quickly reversed, she stepped away and almost turned to run up the sidewalk toward her office.

"Please, in the back. I don't hardly have anybody to chauffeur these days." His voice wavered, softened. "Mrs. One dead. Mrs. Two living in Europe. Mrs. Three I don't know where."

He was asking for indulgence. All right. She could grant that. She got in the back seat of the Cadillac. Oh Lord, could

she still smell Arthur in his place right behind Filmore? No.
She suppressed a sigh. Three years, going on four, yet the car's
interior was still so clean it looked like no one had ever sat on
the back seat. They drove slowly yet smoothly toward the
capitol. He must have driven the route before. Once Filmore
was behind the wheel, he seemed to relax somewhat and, as
the streets were familiar, so did Amy.

There was the pink granite capitol, there was Congress
Avenue in front, a rich snarl of traffic, power shovels, cranes,
pickaxes, the backbone of the downtown area undergoing
major surgery; nearly every building was being restored or
razed to make room for new skyscrapers, and a new wider
sidewalk, still being constructed, meandered down both sides.
Amy was so accustomed to the disorder she hardly noticed it.
Her attention fastened on Filmore. She sensed he would want
her to direct him in some way. That was easy.

"Here." She tapped on the window beside her. "This is
where we stop for lunch. You'll need to circle this block and
maybe the next one."

He nodded then flashed her a smile as someone began
pulling out of a parking place just before they reached the
corner. Arthur used to praise him saying, "I don't know why
but things always open up for Filmore." He'd carry on extrav-
agantly about his chauffeur's luck, not his skill, never for
driving well in bad traffic or avoiding accidents, or slipping
easily into tight parking spots.

When she mentioned this to him, Arthur's reaction was,
"Well, damn it, that's what I pay him for, his skill. But luck!
You can't buy luck!"

"All the same it wouldn't hurt to let him know he's doing
a good job."

She never knew if he took her advice or not. Probably not.
Meeting Arthur right after her divorce when she'd gone home
to New Orleans feeling unloved and lost threw her into a
terribly vulnerable position. He was the sort of man women
tended to like — beguiling, sympathetic. When she no longer

found him kind, his sexual hold on her was broken. By that time she'd gained such a distance from Arthur, she was able to leave him, to return to Texas and the sanity of her work. She was over the flu, over that emotional illness. She pushed aside her life in New Orleans, her memories of Arthur, of Filmore, and those of Rosalie as well. She should have considered Rosalie; they had been close friends, had gone to LSU together. But her whole life had flipped over. She'd left Lousiana the first time with her husband, the second time to fly back to Austin to pick up the pieces of her law practice. Where was Rosalie now? The question drifted though her mind vaguely.

"Just you go ahead. Please, Mrs. Amy. I'll wait here."

"Oh, Filmore." She sighed and refused to scold him. He relied on her to see he couldn't keep his part of the bargain. Hungry and out of sorts, she hardly knew what to do with him. Finally she directed him to a fast food place. She ate her fried chicken in the back seat and was careful not to get a crumb on the white upholstery.

Filmore ate his up front while they sat in the parking lot under a pecan tree that wasn't budding yet.

"What kind of nut is that?" Filmore asked. "I know but I forget."

Amy told him, thinking at the same time that the question could be asked about Filmore. She couldn't humor him forever. Slowly, by careful questioning, she tried to bring him forward a little, to get him to acknowledge the present. He had a son living in New Orleans. More than that he wouldn't say. He evaded all other questions about his son, about grandchildren, about Columbia, a small town in Tennessee where Arthur had another house.

"Built up," was his only reply. Eventually he took her back to the office.

"I enjoyed the . . . the drive, Filmore. Thank you. It's a lovely car."

"Yes'm. I'm glad Mr. Roden left it to me. I look after it good."

"I see you do."

Then he was gone with no promises of return. She went inside and began trying to get in touch with Rosalie. It wasn't easy. At least she did know were to begin calling. She'd known Rosalie for almost twenty years. There were plenty of leads to follow. The hard part was talking to her in Dallas where she was working for a travel agency. No use to dwell on past injuries. Better to get to the point.

"It's me, Amy Wilson."

"Yes?"

All she could hear in the question was curiosity. "I'm calling about — "

"Filmore."

"How did you know?"

"People have told me he's looking for me. Arthur's old friends. When he finds them, he takes them for drives."

"Yes . . . well — "

"So, he took you?"

"Yes."

"I'd rather he didn't find me, Amy. He's harmless, evidently, but he's a little crazy."

"I don't know where the line is between a little crazy and plain crazy."

"I can't say I do either." Rosalie laughed. "I'd appreciate it if you didn't send him my way."

After she'd talked to Rosalie, she felt less isolated. Somehow it helped that other people had the same experience, no matter how strange. Rosalie apparently hadn't held a grudge against her. Too much had happened to both of them. They couldn't stay mad at each other over Arthur Roden.

* * *

For months, for whole seasons, Amy forgot about Filmore, then late in the spring he was back driving up the street by her office and around several blocks two or three times a day, a restless bird looking for a place to light. On a Tuesday, Marialice, frowning ever so slightly because she'd been told about him, showed Filmore in.

"Hello." Amy stood up.

"Hello, Mrs. Amy. You ready to go?"

"Oh . . . Oh, I don't know." She buzzed Marialice and asked for her list of appointments. "Are you going with him, Mrs. Wilson?"

"Yes, I think so."

"You have a full afternoon."

"I know. I just wanted to hear you say so." They both laughed. Marialice's salary had risen as Amy's clients had increased.

"Be careful."

"I will." She put the phone down, picked up her jacket and purse. Following Filmore out, she noticed he looked a little more stooped this time. He seemed to be walking slower.

The Cadillac was as clean, as untouched looking as ever. This time she let him open the back door without an argument. When he was settled behind the wheel, just before he started the motor, she asked, "Around the capitol and down the avenue I suppose?"

"Yes. I know the way."

So around they went threading through the cars parked in a serpentine line on both sides of the street shadowed by the pink granite building. A public monument of the last century, giant poufs of stone billowed as high as hopes for new beginnings, and here she was circling it riding in the last cream-puff car of an artful sensualist, a spoiled rich boy sans noblesse, sans oblige, and finally graceless. Perhaps he had done one good thing by giving the car to his chauffeur. No. Filmore was wasting himself on Arthur's gift. It was of no real use to him. What could he do with it? Take people riding. Since he'd spent most of his life driving white people around, since he was Filmore with one son in the world — and who knew how they got along? — how was he to spend his days? The car had given him a certain independence and had become, at the same time, his mobile jail.

"I . . . don't recognize it, Mrs. Amy. That place you wanted to stop last time."

"Hmm . . . gone I guess." Really, she shouldn't have done it, shouldn't have taken him to a familiar destination that had vanished. She couldn't help wanting to push him forward a little.

"Cities change all the time. Even New Orleans has. Austin has especially. Haven't you noticed? The whole downtown is being rebuilt. They were working on it last year. Don't you remember?"

"Yes'm. I don't like it."

"I know. Lots of people don't. Do you remember the way to the fried chicken place?"

"Yes'm."

"Let's go see if it's still there."

They found it and ate. Filmore sat in the front seat; she remained in back as before. He talked about Foxton, about how old Mr. Arthur had a lake built there for his own convenience and had stocked it with fish and ducks, about the stable full of thoroughbreds which became a garage full of different kinds of cars, some with funny names like Hupmobile and Diana Straight Eight. When he returned her to the office, he seemed reasonably satisfied, placid almost. For the first time Amy asked him his age.

"Late, Mrs. Amy. I'm getting on." He took off his cap, so she could see all of his white hair, "Getting on. Got to be going on home."

"New Orleans?" She stretched out the last syllable as Arthur used to, as Filmore did still.

"I guess."

* * *

"He went to sleep." That's what the police said when they called her.

Filmore's Cadillac had crashed into a concrete bridge railing spanning one of the bayous near a small town west of New Orleans.

"Killed him right away, mam. Pretty near wrecked that Caddy too."

"When?"

"About three this morning. There was a real bad fog. Your card was in his coat pocket."

"His license. Doesn't that tell you anything else?"

"Well, mam, it's the usual. Except the home address given on it turns out to be a golf club up in Tennessee. That's why we had to call you. Thought you might be his lawyer. Thought you might know something else."

"Yes. All right."

What could she tell them? That he was kind, that he was stubborn, that he was an unregenerate conservative, that ghosts rode with him in his car, and none of this would help at all for they wanted something simpler, his son's name. She got it from Rosalie and called the trooper back.

"I'm sorry to tell you, mam. But this wouldn't have happened if he'd been on the interstate. He was driving down an old road that everybody used to take into New Orleans."

She knew the narrow curving road which twisted over bayous, wandered across moss strewn, kudzu-covered half jungles, ambled through one-stoplight towns. Anger over the predictability of his death, anger at herself for her failure to deter him, flickered in her mind. She thanked the trooper and put the receiver down. It was still quite early in the morning, and in the silence she could almost hear Arthur cursing. "God-amighty!" That was what he said. "God-amighty!" she repeated aloud to her empty office.

Overlappings

ET'S GO DOWN to the corral. It's been a long time since I watched Leo shear." Bern walked across the room to the door.

Annie looked up at him. "You know we can't. They'll talk. The others will even if Leo doesn't."

"So they will talk. I'm tired of being in the house."

"With me?"

"No. I'm only tired of being inside." She watched him go. He refused to listen to her. He would do as he pleased unless she could prevent him, and she couldn't. Because he'd changed the rules. She realized that when he called from Mexico City. This time she, not Leo, had to meet his plane. The demand was flattering. It was also a way of forcing her to decide.

* * *

When Annie didn't return from the ranch at the expected time, Cliff waited a while then called the foreman. She was a woman who generally moved according to schedule, a more flexible one now that the children had gone to college. Still she usually came home when she said she would. He did likewise although he was known to miss a plane when a meeting ran late. His call to Poke was unsatisfactory.

33

"Last time I seen her, Cliff, was when I took her back to the house around dinnertime yesterday. I was down at the corral till about three. Had the doctoring to do and the marking. We're short thirty-eight goats, and I've been riding all the pastures looking — "

For more years than Cliff could remember Poke had worked for Annie's parents. Now, he often said, what was left of him worked for Annie. Accustomed to his meanderings as he was to his taciturnity, Cliff let Poke talk about goats for sometime before he broke in. "I spoke to her about eight-thirty last night, maybe a little before. She said she was driving back this morning. I've already checked with the highway patrol. They haven't seen anything of her, not that they would ordinarily. It's six now. Take a look at the house for me. No one answers out there, but that phone doesn't always work."

When he hung up he wondered why he'd been so slow to begin searching. Annie wasn't an adventurous woman. She was fond of the ranch though and liked to spend a night out there alone occasionally. Every fall and spring she drove up to oversee the goat shearing, not that much overseeing was required.

* * *

"I thought you were going down to the corral. Why did you come back so soon, Bern?"

"Poke's there. His truck is parked on the other side of the barn."

"We're out behind the barn." Her laughter rose and just as quickly subsided. "Thanks for — "

"That's all right. I'll see Leo at the noon break."

"Now I have to go to the corral."

"I know. La patrona."

It was true. She was la patrona though all she did was sit on the fence and watch. The shearers were more careful when she was around. Fewer goats were nicked. Fewer wisps of mohair drifted out to the pasture. She liked seeing the men work,

34

liked seeing them peel away the heavy, dirty coats. "Bern, I always — "

"I thought you were tired of always."

"I am and I'm not. If staying here hurts your latino pride so much, come with me. Let Poke see you, let him talk."

"Oh, Annie. Shut up. Shut up. You'll make us both angry if you keep talking." He caught her by her arms, held on a moment, then let go.

* * *

Alvarez was the head of the shearing crew. Leo Alvarez, Bern's younger brother. Honest, Cliff was certain. He made his men keep correct count of the number they sheared and worked alongside them. Some locals, some wetbacks. Nothing to worry about there. All the ranchers around Mullin used him. Annie loved to see Leo's truck running up the low hill to the corral. "It looks like an ancient rickety shearing machine, something Don Quixote might have imagined rising out of those dusty Spanish plains, Cliff. The panels tilt madly and that old faded pink canvas he still uses flaps in the wind. Everything jolts, and rattles, and squeaks. Then three or four men crawl out of the truck, all of them grinning." Anything strange tickled her, the sight of domestic ducks mingling with wild ones on the lake, a red oak tree that kept its leaves all through November, a peculiar question from one of the children, any foreign place. She'd loved Mexico ever since she'd gone to school down there, so they went back in the summers and took the children with them to Guanajuato, Oaxaca, Jalapa, anywhere it was cool and they could rent a house. Yet she also liked the things she knew. She kept the customs, particularly at the ranch. The Sawyers ran cattle mostly. They had run goats too for nearly ten years, so Annie wanted to keep on even though she'd left the ranch at eighteen, the same age he'd left Mullin. The Sawyers . . . both of them were gone. Except for a few aunts and uncles, he was Annie's family now. The ranch was her one real tie to the past, and he had encouraged her going out there when maybe he shouldn't have. But how could he keep her in Austin when she so obviously wanted to go?

* * *

Annie stopped in the hall where pictures of her parents hung. She hadn't really looked at them for months. There was the only picture her mother had made of herself wearing a hat, a green tilted straw with a huge brim and a bunch of cherries dangling. Glossy, dark red cherries, she could still see the color though the picture was black and white. She'd thought they were real at first. What was it Mother said? Yes. "Your father goes around in a hat all the time. I thought I'd have the photograph made to remind him I have a hat to wear." She didn't have many occasions to wear an outrageous hat in Mullin County. All one spring she wore it when she went shopping in Austin or San Antonio until Daddy begged her to buy another one. How she used to worry about Mother not coming home from San Antonio . . . so far from Mullin she had to spend the night. The picture had been taken at a studio there. Afterward she put the hat away. She hadn't known a defiant gesture when she saw one. Oh well, she was just ten and it was only a gesture, a shadow of her mother's longing for city life, for something richer. The rest she stifled the way some ranch women planted rose bushes, those one-summer blooms which they knew the next drought would wither. What contrary moves we insist on making sometimes. One step forward, one step back.

"What are you doing, Annie?"

"Looking at Mother's picture, thinking about her life out here. She loved this place and hated it too sometimes. She didn't grow up on a ranch. She was from San Antonio."

"Let me see." Bern stood beside her in the dark hall in front of the walnut chest with its cracked marble top. "She was beautiful." He sighed. "My mother never had a hat like that."

"Not many women did. I guess that's why she bought it."

36

* * *

Cliff caught himself reciting worries the way other people recited prayers. The Sawyer place was remote, a mile and a half to the nearest neighbor, and there were plenty of natural dangers — rattlesnakes, coral snakes, copperheads, scorpions, wasps, spiders — he'd killed a black widow in the tack room the last time they were there — three horses that ran wild in the pasture where the house was, a lame bull in the same pasture. Ah, he was letting his imagination run wild. Anything could happen anytime. Annie was careful. She was safer on home territory than she was on the highway. But she would call, wouldn't she? Or have somebody call. If it was car trouble, he'd know by now. What kind of trouble could she be in? Everything had seemed all right last night. But wasn't that the way he wanted to think? To throw a reassuring net over all. Annie accused him of that when he tried to comfort her at times.

* * *

"Why are you calling Cliff?"

"It's hard to give up the things I've been doing for twenty years."

"What I believe you mean is it's hard to give up Cliff. You still love him."

"Of course I do. Don't expect me to give up loving Cliff. There are many kinds of love, Bern. You know that." She sighed. There were so few words for emotions, for love, for grief. Only anger produced a lot of words, and all of them the wrong ones. Much of her time with Bern was misspent arguing. They had so little time, a few days each year, and every day he always said she must do as he asked . . . when she was not ready to. When Anita was alive they were peaceful . . . in the summers. In the mountain towns where she'd rented houses all over Mexico, and they had come to visit. Then at the beaches Bern loved where he and Anita insisted she and Cliff must visit them, must bring the children, must give way and let the servants wait on them. Because it was Mexico.

That was what Anita used to say, "You must not take their work from them, Annie." She had to remind her every time.

"I have to make this call, Bern. I'll say what I usually say. I'll tell Cliff how many pounds were sheared."

"All right. I'll wait for you on the porch. I can see from here the moon is coming out of the clouds."

* * *

The connection was bad. Cliff had to ask Evelyn to repeat herself.

"I said she's not out there. Poke just phoned from the ranch to ask me to tell you."

"Why didn't he call me from the ranch?"

"You know how he is about long distance. He hates to dial it. Says there's too many numbers. He always leaves one out."

"Well, is there anything, any sign of where she might be?"

"I don't know how to explain this. The car is in front of the house, but all her stuff is gone. Poke says the house looks real neat. Locked up too."

"I don't guess there was any — "

"There's a mirror propped up against one end of the couch over by the door like she meant to take it with her and forgot."

"Don't touch anything out there, Evelyn. Tell Poke not to either."

"All right. Cliff, I'm sorry."

"For what?"

"Whatever. I hope she hasn't come to any harm."

"Did Poke see signs of any other cars?"

"I don't know. I should have asked him."

"Evelyn, when Poke gets there, see that he calls me."

"All right."

She sounded shaken. He was shaken himself. He would have to call the police now to report Annie was missing. They wouldn't even begin to look for her for twenty-four hours after he called. He'd have to convince them she'd been gone that long already. Should call the sheriff in Lampasas too. The

ranch house was in that county. First — before calling anybody — he'd have to hear more from Poke. Damn his foolishness about the phone. Probably had to get Evelyn to dial for
him. At least he was sharp-eyed. He would notice every little
detail. Used to tell him he'd make a good witness. Could she
have been kidnapped? Why? A forty-year-old woman. Forty-
two. Pretty still. Not especially rich. The land was worth a
lot, but she'd never sell it. Crazies didn't care. Don't look at
today's paper. Don't check on who's been raped, robbed,
beaten, stabbed, murdered in one day. It all happens everyday. Don't think about the damned cases . . . the client whose
son disappeared, the woman with all the knife wounds, the —
Don't! Wait. Have a drink, have two. Wait for Poke to call.

* * *

"Why the mirror?" Bern ran a finger around the frame as if
checking the finish for flaws.

"It was my mother's."

"Yes, all right. Why do you want to take it with you?"

"See the little holes in the frame? They were made by my
father's shotgun. When I was a child he brought it into the
house loaded. He never did that again. The glass was shat-
tered. Mother replaced it, but she kept the damaged frame."

"Was he shooting at her?"

"No. What a crazy idea. It was momentary carelessness.
That's all. He was putting the gun on its rack. He'd forgotten
there was a shell in the chamber. When he lifted it up, it
slipped. His hand caught the trigger. Shot sprayed through the
mirror and all around it on the bedroom wall. Haven't you
ever noticed?"

"No. And you haven't told me why you want to take it."

"I'm leaving everything else." She was leaving her familiar
place and going to his and she wanted to take a piece of her
own with her. Was that it? Or was she merely a woman running out of a burning house choosing something indiscrimi-
nately? No. That couldn't be true. She'd always chosen with
great care — Bern, Cliff, Bern.

39

* * *

Poke Rabbin stood on the steps of the house Annie had been raised in. The sun had already set. All that was left was the show. Enough dust for a good one too. Red and pink clouds smeared the southwestern rim of the sky. When she was little Annie had ridden off that way to school every morning. He'd gone with her, watched her catch the bus, then taken the pony home. In the afternoon they repeated the trip, and when the weather got bad either he or Bob made it down and back in the pickup with her. Neither one of them minded. It was part of the routine on the place like calving, or feeding, or fencing. Only he liked going after Annie better than doing any of the rest. He and Evelyn should have had a bunch of kids but they couldn't, so he got to share Annie, the only one Bob and Catherine had. She showed an early preference for men. Never wanted to stay in the kitchen and let Catherine teach her how to bake cookies. If he and Bob went hunting, she went with them. He'd taught her how to shoot a .22 first, then a .410, and even if she didn't like deer hunting, she knew how to handle a 30-30. Bob said a girl ought to know which end of a gun to point. When Annie was twelve — too young, Evelyn said — Bob taught her how to drive, gave her an old cranky Ford to get herself to the gate in. How long was it after that that the Alvarez boy showed up? A year or so. He started giving her rides home from school. Just to the gate. He was two or three years older than she was, and he knew he wasn't supposed to go no further. What was that boy's name? Bernie? No. Bernado, and everybody called him Bern. Leo Alvarez' oldest brother. Sometimes Leo was with them when they drove to the gate in that beat-up truck.

Pulling out his tin of tobacco before he sat down, Poke lifted out just enough with one finger. Like an old goat chewing, Evelyn used to say. Then she got used to it and gave up on reforming him. He sat on the second step and put his elbows against the top step. He didn't like none of what was probably going to happen next, and he had to think on it. Replacing the tobacco, he patted his back pocket to make sure the letter Annie had left was still there. He'd hand it over to Cliff himself. Damned if he'd read a private letter to anybody over the long-distance telephone.

* * *

"Annie, why are you writing?"

"I have to let him know something, or he'll think — "

"What?"

"He'll think something disastrous has happened, Bern."

"I didn't know Cliff had such an imagination."

"Why not? Most people imagine something when a person disappears. Remember, even if he's not a criminal lawyer a lot of people with criminal problems come to him first."

"And — ?"

"He listens. Later he refers them to someone else."

"You don't like for me to talk about Cliff, do you?"

"Sometimes you underestimate him."

"It's the weakness of a jealous man."

"Do you want to read what I've written?"

"To Cliff? No . . . Yes. No."

* * *

Poke moved up to the top step, wrapped his fingers around his bony knees, and watched the afterglow. It couldn't last. Annie and the Alvarez boy. At least he hadn't told on them. Talk made its way and gossip traveled fastest. Bob told her no more riding around with the Mexican boy. We like them fine, but Anglos and Mexicans don't mix here.

"She said I was prejudiced, Poke. I told her damn right I was. The Alvarezes are shearers, always will be. They're Mexicans, always will be. What else was I to tell her?"

He groaned inwardly. His daddy was a cowboy. He was a foreman. Everybody didn't stay the same. Bern was smart, smarter than a lot of the ranchers' sons. Most of them hated him for it too.

"What did Annie say then?"

41

"She said things didn't have to stay the same. I told her to wait awhile and see."

They quit riding around together. Saw each other at school, at other places, he reckoned. She wasn't his daughter, still having no children, Annie was, in some way his. He was as relieved as Bob when Bern went off. Some of his mother's people lived in Mexico still. He graduated top of his class from Mullin High School, went to college in Mexico City. Half the people in Mullin never dreamed there was a college down there. Leo stayed home, took over the shearing when his daddy died. Of course Annie went away to college too. Hated to see her leave. Seemed like there were big holes in the days when she was gone.

After that there was a lot of her life he knew nothing about. Had to be. She came home Thanksgiving, Christmas, Easter. In the summers she was gone way off — Europe, Mexico. Somewhere down there, a place where there was a summer school, San Miguel . . . that was it. To learn Spanish better, she said. Was that when it happened? Did she pick up with Bern Alvarez again that summer? If she did, then why did she come back and marry Cliff the next October? Of course she'd always known him. Everybody knew Cliff Mullin. Town was named after his granddaddy.

* * *

"Do you mind leaving all this?" Bern waved his arm to indicate the living room, the hearth, the old branding irons, the pictures of her grandparents in florid gilt frames on the wall, the furniture so carved in claws and curls that sometimes she was reminded of hulking animals sleeping . . . griffins, bears, lions. The zoo, her children called it, the museum, her mother said, because Daddy liked the room as Grandmother had left it.

"Do you mind leaving your house, your ranch?"

"No. It will still be here, and it will still be mine, and one day it will belong to my children."

42

"Then leave the mirror."

But it was where she saw herself. Wasn't that why she chose
it . . . to remember her father's accident, the shattering, the
replacement. Wasn't that what she was doing? How carefully
we choose things even when choosing unknowingly. By marrying Cliff, I stayed close to Bern. So? So, I have known that
for a long time.

"Can't you give it up, Annie? It will be awkward to carry."

"All right." Do we ever truly leave? Has he ever really left?
Will I? Am I the part of his past he chooses to take with him?
Or do I choose him because he's part of mine? Memory is
oppressive here. Maybe that's why I can go.

* * *

Poke stood up, stretched, and looked over at the windmill.
Running too fast before the light south wind. Blades whirling
free in the air. Not a damn drop was being pumped. Sucker
rod broke probably. He'd have to get hold of Patterson to work
on it tomorrow.

He swung the door to his pickup shut, spat out the window,
and drove into Mullin where Evelyn met him at the kitchen
door.

"Cliff wants you to call him."

"She left a letter."

"I thought she might."

"What do you know about all this?"

"Not much more than you've put together probably." Evelyn sighed. "Only I can't . . . I can't quite figure it out. Maybe
if you read Cliff the letter — "

"No. It's got his name on it. He has to read it himself. Call
him for me, Evelyn. Tell him I'll meet him at Seward Junction."

"That's way over halfway for you."

"I didn't arrange the towns around here. Anyway he'll have
to wade through all that Sunday night traffic coming and going
out of Austin. Tell him to meet me at that filling station there."

43

"Did you see any signs of — ?"

"Like I told you. The place was real neat. Only the mirror on the floor. Couldn't tell anything by the road. Too dry and too windy to hold tracks. Besides the shearers was in and out yesterday. Annie drove that same road. So did I. Everything's all mixed up."

"Sure is." Evelyn smiled. "Don't be too upset, Poke. It was bound to happen sometime. Go on and get your supper while I phone Clifford."

All the way to Seward Junction he wondered what she meant. Evelyn had a whole mysterious-woman side to her he'd never been able to figure out. What was bound to happen? He'd intended to ask her, but was so hungry he'd let the remark pass.

* * *

Annie stood at the window watching the windmill blades blur together. It was moving too fast. Sucker rod was probably broken. She could call Patterson, the windmill man, to come out. Poke would notice and call him tomorrow when he came by to check on the goats. It was a sound she'd miss. Had Bern ever missed the sound of a windmill turning? She doubted he had. Bern disdained nearly everything in Mullin, Texas, not everyone though, not his family. He saw them each time. Leo met his plane and took him home for a day or so. They believed he returned to Mexico. Instead he came to her at the ranch. Someone always had to be fooled. Her parents first, now his, and for the last five years, Cliff. She'd never liked the deceit. It was the price she paid for wavering, a common guilt, and she was weary of it.

They could be direct, but it was sometimes difficult. They responded to each other so quickly, too quickly often. Everything was easier when they were in bed. They were still good for each other even after how many years? Almost twenty she'd been married to Cliff. What a fury Bern had been in when he discovered they were getting married. It was as if he'd been betrayed. In a way, he was.

44

The phone call from Mexico was brief.

"Why are you marrying him?"

"Cliff's a kind man, and he loves me."

"You don't love him. You love me."

"Living in Mexico has changed you. You're harder to like."

"What has liking to do with it?"

"Everything."

The wires hummed through the thick silences between their words. He hadn't called since she'd left. What was she to think? She had believed. . . . Oh, she'd believed he'd become impossible. Once he'd gone to Mexico City he was quickly involved in machismo, that ridiculous strut, that cock-a-whammy version of male dominance. She hadn't realized how much solace he needed. Neither all his intelligence, nor all her attention, nor Cliff's steady friendship could save him from Mullin's careless tongues mumbling "Meskin." So he became Mexican truly and turned his back on the gringos.

What did he look like then? All she could see was the tall, thin young man, always wearing sunglasses, always dressed in white, always demanding. He had consumed her summer. When she refused to go to him in Mexico City anymore, he came to San Miguel. Flowers everyday, music two or three times a week — mariachis, violinists, and once two Indians playing reed flutes so plaintively she wanted to laugh and cry. The songs were alike though. Sometimes harsh, sometimes tender, all were outpourings of grief over the pain of love.

A part of courtship in Mexico, everyone told her. Yet she mistrusted such effusion. He would ask her to meet his family next if he was serious, they said without knowing who he was, without knowing she had already met his family in Mullin, Texas, where his father and brother sheared her father's goats. In San Miguel her friends knew only his aunt and uncle, Lena Alvarez's brother, a successful coffee merchant from Jalapa who kept an apartment in Mexico City.

"Marry me!" cried the trumpets, the guitars, the violins,

the flutes, the pink gladiolus, the yellow daisies, the roses of every color. She had refused. He was volatile, demanding, and after she'd slept with him, arrogant. He seemed to think he could plan their whole lives alone. "We will live in the city, have a house on the coast. In the summers we will — "

"Sometime we have to go back to Texas."

"No. Let them come down here."

"My parents will never — "

"Yes they will."

"You don't know my father."

"He is a proud man, and he has only one child. He will come to Mexico."

"I'm not so sure of that."

"If he won't, your mother will."

"My mother does as my father wishes."

"I wish you would be more like her."

"I have no intention of being like my mother. You are not like your father. Why should I copy my mother?"

Their quarrel grew and spread like the bougainvillea whose tenuous leaves turned to red flames flickering over the patio wall. So she left, went back to Austin to finish her last year at the university, to see Cliff Mullin graduate from law school, to marry him. Because she would not allow herself to marry Bern? Wasn't it a question of her own pride? Taught to think and act for herself, she could not imagine being half of a cock and hen pair.

Now, twenty years later they had become a pair. Impossible to explain. Cliff would never believe her. He believed in explanations, in reasons. There was one she could think of, but it was too unsatisfactory, too indefinite to give him. She had grown up alone and so, essentially, had Bern. There was no one remotely like him in his family. When she joined him, they returned together to their solitudes which like feathers, like fans, overlapped.

46

* * *

Evelyn straightened up her kitchen quickly after Poke left. She was tired of kitchen work, worn out with pots, and pans, and decisions about meals. At sixty-nine she guessed she had a right to be though it seemed to her she remembered being tired of all that when she was thirty-five or forty. Most women she knew got that way unless they were crazy about cooking. Like her, they kept on throwing it all together. Poke was good to help out even if he wasn't much on planning ahead. He was a fried egg and ham cook. The one who really planned ahead was Annie. She came up to the ranch with menus made and all the food cooked. Because, she said, "I don't want to have to think about it for two or three days." She remembered Annie's determined voice. But she couldn't plan ahead for everything. Too much happened, too many other people made plans of their own. Like Clifford. He was patient. He knew how to wait.

Most of Mullin came to that wedding. People drove up from Austin and from ranches all over Texas. It was a natural match. Sawyers and Mullins, ranchers and bankers, only Cliff was breaking away to be a lawyer. Well there was only room for so many on the land and in the banks, and he had three brothers. The minute Annie married Cliff, Bern Alvarez married a girl he knew in Mexico. Leo told her, shook his head when he did.

Of all the Alvarezes she knew Leo best. He sheared her six goats twice a year. They'd talk while he worked out in the corral. Leo, kneeling on a board, worked slowly because he was talking.

"My brother is a fool about Annie. It was right for her to marry Cliff."

"I don't know."

"Her parents wanted it."

"Sometimes Bob and Catherine, like a lot of other people, want what they think is best, and it isn't. But who am I to say?"

47

Leo shrugged. "Who is anyone? I know well as you about Bern and Annie."

"Something must have happened while she was in San Miguel."

Leo smiled, his clippers held in mid-air for a moment. "Si."

It was the one Spanish word he permitted himself around Anglos.

"They quarreled I guess."

Leo nodded, untied his goat, and reached for another one. "Here she is the daughter of a rich man."

"She put on airs?"

"Not so much, but you know Annie. She gets her way. Maybe — "

"Maybe Bern wanted his way in his country."

Leo laughed.

She could still imagine him. Young, not so fat then, dark-headed, careful. Almost twenty years ago, on his knees in the corral, laughing. Leo fit into his family, wanted to carry on when his father died. He'd always planned to. Nobody knew Bern's plans. He didn't look like the rest of them. Had Lena Alvarez . . . ? No use making up tales about some other woman. Lena said Bern favored her side of the family, and who could deny it since all of them lived in Mexico still. Bern went back to his mother's people where he stayed, and according to Leo, he prospered.

"He's an engineer, Mrs. Rabbin. He takes care of the oil while I," he held both arms wide apart, "I take care of the goats."

Did he mind the difference in them? He didn't seem to. She ran into him at the feed store right after the big well erupted into the Bay of Campeche.

"Bern's down there. He's got plenty of trouble now. We won't get a visit from him for awhile." He smiled. "Which is worse, do you think, to smell of goats or oil?"

She said she hardly knew and smiled back at him. Though neither of them admitted it, they both knew Bern flew in every fall and spring when Annie's goats were sheared. She hadn't gone out to the ranch snooping. She seldom went to the place at all when Annie was there. Maybe she was jealous. Poke had always protected Annie so . . . ever since she was a little kid. He was doing that now, keeping still, waiting. Because he hadn't told anybody about Bern's trips up, hadn't even told her. She'd found out by accident. Driving back from Lampasas in March, five years ago. The highway went right down by the airport, such a small landing strip, only big enough for private planes, and who was that? Leo Alvarez hugging a man taller than he was. Then she recalled the date. Shearing time at the Sawyers' wasn't it? Bern wasn't flying up just to visit his family. If he was she'd see him in town and she didn't. Leo never mentioned his visits. Neither did any of the others. So Bern and Annie had been carrying on five years at least. How many more? What happened to his wife . . . anything? Leo hadn't said, and she wasn't of a mind to ask. Did Clifford know, or did he keep himself from knowing? Did he know and not know at the same time? Hard to tell about Cliff. He was a button-lip like Poke, like most of the men she knew. Whatever bothered them the most, they hid the most.

Wonder if Clifford had called the police? Of course she was too curious. Hard not to be even though it was a small secret so far. She and Poke knew. The Alvarezes? Bern must see all of them when he flew up. Probably he didn't tell them anything. It took four or five hours to shear Annie's goats. She didn't have many over three hundred. They ran mainly cows and calves. Bern could stay out of sight at the house. After the shearing he'd be free to roam anywhere on ten thousand acres.

Did he like it? Did Bern Alvarez like the country he'd been raised in? Annie did and didn't. Too dry, she said. Too hot in the summer, too rocky, and there were way too many snakes, she complained after she'd moved to Austin. But she knew how to look at a thing another way. There was a fairness about Annie. When they were talking that time she'd said, "Evelyn, you've done what my mother did. You've endured the droughts, the heat, ridden over the rocks, and killed the snakes."

"I don't believe we'll ever get them all killed."

They both laughed.

"Maybe I like it here, Annie, because I haven't lived any-wheres else. Maybe it's because I only know this part of Texas, so it's all right with me. People get used to their places."

True enough for her, not for Annie. She was restless. Bob and Catherine sent her to Europe for a whole year before she made that trip to Mexico. Sounded like from what she'd said she didn't much want to come home.

"You ought to see the cowboys in France way down in the south and the ranches in Spain. Splendid! Especially the ones where they raise the fighting bulls."

She went on and on about France and Spain, but she didn't have much to say about Mexico when she got back. San Miguel was cool, pretty, yes, there were lots of churches, and she'd learned real Spanish. That was about all. Then just as the heat was breaking in late October she married Cliff. Must have been something . . . something unfinished between Annie and Bern, or maybe it couldn't be finished.

* * *

Cliff waited on the asphalt drive running around the station at Seward Junction, a nonplace almost. There was a shack advertising barbeque. He and Annie had tried it once.

"The old Texas con game," Annie said. "Bake it, throw bottled sauce on it, and make passing strangers pay for it." They paid and went out the door leaving the greasy meat, canned beans, and gelatinous cole slaw sinking in the paper plates. In later years they laughed as they passed by. Seward Junction became their code term for bad food, a private joke, the kind a lot of married people had. They had a number of them, but he couldn't put his mind on one more at the moment. He kept drifting off like a weak radio signal to return to a single question: Was she all right?

There, swinging in beside him, Poke's truck. Both of them

got out at the same time. Poke met him at the tailgate of the pickup and handed him the note wordlessly as if it was an ordinary transaction, as if he was handing him a bill for feed or a list of calves just sold. Nodding as he took it, Cliff returned to his car.

Dear Cliff, I'm all right. I had to leave. I'm sorry to hurt you. There doesn't seem to be a way out of that. I'll call you later. Love, Annie

He reread trying to make sense of the words which wriggled together under the car's interior yellow light. Poke was waiting, leaning against his pickup's door. He appeared to be merely watching the road. Cliff folded the note precisely in the same places Annie had and put it back in the envelope. For a moment he stared blankly out the windshield. A moth bumped against the window. He switched the light off. He'd known it was possible, had known before they married, and put it out of mind.

"Poke."

"Yep."

"It's just as well I didn't call the police. She's . . . she's all right."

Poke studied the asphalt as if he were looking for a map in it. "Guess I'll be getting on back then."

"Thanks for coming."

"Sure."

He stood by the car while Poke turned his pickup around. Funny. Neither one of them mentioned it, yet both of them knew Annie had left with Bern Alvarez. Maybe he was the only one she'd ever really loved. How could . . . ? No. It couldn't be so. They had two children, twenty years together, a lot of life. Maybe she had loved them both. And how much was merely circumstance? If her father hadn't been so foolish, hadn't tried to break up an adolescent romance between his daughter and a Mexican boy, would Annie be home right now? What if he and Bern hadn't been friends? What if he hadn't helped him? For a year, the year Annie was sixteen, he'd picked her up at the ranch, gone after her in his own car, then delivered her to Bern. And fallen in love with her himself. He'd had to wait all that time. Had to wait for all of them to grow up. Had to wait until he was finished with law school and Annie came back from Mexico free at last of Bern . . . or said she was.

* * *

"Annie, he will guess you're with me."

"Certainly." Why do we have to go on talking about Cliff? Do we take him with us this way? Is that what he wants to do, to make Cliff an accomplice once more?

"I've chosen to live with you. You wanted me to make the choice."

"Sometimes I feel a little guilty. That's all." Sometimes he seemed too interested in Cliff's responses, too curious about another man's opinion.

"Look how blue — the ocean and the sky. They're almost one."

"Yes. A blue bowl. We'll be flying over Yucatan soon. See, we're above land again."

From the plane it looked like there were only two or three roads on the whole peninsula. Odd. She supposed there wasn't much to go to and from. Mérida and what else? The islands . . . Cozumel, Cancun. But she couldn't see Mérida. There would be roads to and from the ruins, to Chichén Itzá, and Uxmal surely. Bern was concentrating. Long flight . . . one country to another, one man to another. She'd known only two, loved just two. Why? Other women, some of her own friends, the ones she grew up with, fell in and out of love all the time while she'd continually been the point of a triangle. She knew Cliff too well . . . they'd had everything in common. And Bern? She'd never truly known him. When they were growing up, she thought she did. They were strangers now. What had she done? What had she done? Run away, of course. Anyone could see that. She could have been more discreet if she hadn't been sick of discretion.

* * *

Cliff started the motor and pulled out on the highway blinking his eyes at the rapidly moving traffic. Highway 183, where Annie's parents were killed eight years ago. If they were alive would Annie be home now? No. She would have gone even if they were, if she wanted to, if she was ready to. Damn that truck. Why was it weaving in and out of lanes? Why hadn't he been noticing? Lulled. He'd let himself be lulled by normality. Someone would have to write and tell the children. Dear Matthew, Your mother has run off with one of my old friends. Dear Katie, Your mother has gone to live in Mexico with Bern Alvarez who she prefers to me. Oh, no. Annie, you must explain it to them. It's not my job. I'm paid to straighten out other people's messes, not yours.

* * *

Bern's hand was on her shoulder. Annie looked around at the airport. Lots of glass, lots of polished onyx. The floors were covered with it like the airport at Oaxaca only at Oaxaca you could see the mountains in the distance and here it was tropical . . . hibiscus, crotan, jasmine, bougainvillea, banana trees, and the smell . . . always it smelled the same. Cheap tobacco, and something they mopped the floors with, something chemical, and dust.

"I decided to bring you to Cancun instead of to Mexico because I was afraid you'd want to leave me immediately if we went to the city."

"Why should I — ?"

"You haven't really been to Mexico for almost twenty years. You took the train from the border to San Miguel, flew to Mexico and changed planes to go everywhere else. For twenty years you've only seen the airport. The city has become a different place."

"Overcrowding, pollution — I've read about it."

53

"Yes. So I had to bring you here first. If you don't like the condo . . . if you don't like the way it's decorated, you can change it to suit you."

As she had thought. Anita's ghost to deal with. Well she would deal with it in time.

"I don't quite understand where we are, Bern. How far from the airport is the island?"

"We're already on the island. We have to drive a few miles before you can see water again."

* * *

For too long he'd looked forward to too little. Cliff recognized his middle-aged complaint. Had Annie felt it too? Had she run off in search of change? What was that over there? A new supermarket? Yes. More traffic to pull in and out of the road, and there were too many access lanes already, too many possibilities for catastrophe. He'd never learned to keep alert enough to see his own approaching. Matter of lack of imagination or will? Or both? Well, he couldn't go looking for disaster every morning, he had to live beside it unknowing. He should have known, should have guessed something when Bern lost Anita. Freakish. What had an earthquake in Mexico City to do with us? Everything. How was it she died? A collapsing balcony? Flowerpots falling off a balcony? Annie would remember. She's not home, you fool! She's somewhere in Mexico with my childhood friend Bernado Alvarez whose wife was murdered by a falling flowerpot. The chain of circumstance is so long . . . stretching from Mexico to me. And old . . . running through generations of Alvarezes, Mullins, and Sawyers. And there's something more than circumstance . . . something else entirely . . . Turn. The place to turn. Almost forgot after years of making it. All my life spent defining, analyzing, arguing, what is the one word I want? What is it she finds in Bern she's never found in me? Passion? No. I felt it, and so did she. Intensity? Perhaps it's his intensity. He has enough to match her own. That's why she married me

54

twenty years ago, to let me shelter her from Bern. She came
to me for calm. Annie and I . . . most of the time we were
peaceful together. Turn again. The last turn. The house will
be empty. Children gone. She wait? Yes, she waited till they
were in college. Used to tease her when Bern's letters came.
We sent condolences after Anita was killed. He sent back love
letters. In every one he spoke of unhappiness. Misery covered
pages. Women love to comfort.

"He'll be up here after you." I warned her when I should
have warned myself.

"Ah, Cliff. He's only lonely. He'll find another wife in
Mexico I'm sure."

Was she dissembling? Not at first. Later? Perhaps. Better
not to know. Is that why Poke didn't say anything. He knew?
Ignorance, my wonderful shield. All the lights are on. What
can I do now? Why can't I be angry? It would help if I could
be angry. He went inside and turned the lights off all over the
house. When he reached their bedroom, he lay down on the
bed completely clothed waiting for the shock to wear thin,
waiting for the first wave of grief to hit.

* * *

"Bern, I must. I said I would."

"We've just gotten here."

"I was supposed to be home this morning. He's probably
frantic even if he did get my note."

"Cliff? He's never been frantic in his life."

"You don't know. You haven't been living with him." She
walked to a window and looked out at the sun dipping into the
sea. "Either I do what I feel must be done, or nothing will
work out. Right now . . . whatever I have to do, I don't want
to argue about it."

He put his hands lightly on her shoulders. "All right. Of
course."

"Could you send a wire for me? Here, I've written it out.
Fill in the number, please." She handed him a slip of paper

55

with a blank left for the telephone number. "I said I'd call, but nothing will be accomplished that way. If he wants he can call. I owe him that."

"And you will write?"

"Yes. Now."

He nodded.

Somehow she had to be outside to write. She chose a small balcony overlooking the ocean. On one side a white sand beach curved away to an infinite point and on the other, the beach curved toward her. Afterglow pinked the clouds, turned the water dark blue.

Dear Cliff, I'm on Cancun an island off the coast of Quintana Roo on the Yucatán Peninsula north of Cozumel. This place wasn't even on the map when we were growing up. Did it matter? The names of islands, their exact geographic locations? She'd always thought so, had wanted to know them, a habit she couldn't change though she'd changed everything else in her life. Cliff would want to know. He was an exact man. *Bern has a condominium here.*

I know I said I would call, however, I thought it best to write, and easier, I will confess. I regret leaving as I did. I don't, but it won't help to say so. It was the only way I would go.

Of course you will want a divorce. Of course I am the one who needs it. *Do you want to file there, or would it be better for me to get one here?* He's the injured one. Best to let him decide.

I will write to the children, and I hope you will also. Let us try not to use them. Katie is twenty, and Matt is nineteen. They are both old enough to lead their own lives even if they fail to understand mine. It was really too much to ask she was sure. What child ever knew its mother's true personality? To them she was Mother, slightly scandalous now but still Mother. Their lives had been so different from hers. They were city children. They took music lessons, went to swim meets, riding classes, dances, painting classes, summer camp, winter vacations at ski resorts, summers in the mountains and on the beaches of Mexico, and when they were home the house swarmed with children. She grew up in the solitude her mother had grown accustomed to. She'd learned how to shoot, to ride, and to swim so awkwardly she had to have lessons when she was sixteen. Except for Poke and Evelyn and her parents, there were a few aunts and uncles, some friends, not many until high school. Then there were Bern and Cliff. After them no one else, no other man was interesting. She had never known another person like Bern. He was both a part of her past and foreign to it. And Cliff had linked them and she. . . .

She held her unfinished letter in one hand and looked out at the little waves lapping against the shore.

Save These Instructions

When you can't buy shoes to fit:

 N MADRID in 1956, she and her husband were wedged in a hotel elevator on their way to a restaurant on the roof. As usual when riding elevators, she looked down at the floor. She had on her best shoes, a pair of black suede high-heels, size nine triple A. The stocky heels rose two inches and the toes were rounded. "Baby doll toes," they were called. All around her stood a crowd of Spanish women wearing shoes equally black though much smaller. Nobody wore a shoe above a size five and their toes were pointed, quite pointed, as were their heels. They were trim, fashionable, sharp-looking women. For a moment she felt much too large, rather frumpy, and decidedly foolish. All over the western world women were probably wearing pointed-toed shoes, and she had realized it only then.

Throughout her life this ridiculous scene would replay itself in her head for no known reason just as a number of others did. That the sight of all those pointed shoes in the elevator automatically made her feel awkward and dowdy hardly seemed important later. It was a minor humiliation, something bound to happen in any woman's life at least once like the everlasting joke about being caught with curlers in your hair. To have missed a major fashion change was no great loss.

She wasn't the type of woman who noticed or followed every trend; however, it was true she replaced the round-toed shoes with pointed-toed ones when she returned to the U.S. in 1957. She had no memory of being unhappy with them until the scene in the Madrid elevator. Perhaps her memory of the situation was faulty. Perhaps it replayed because she had cried about her feet, so long and narrow, so impossibly American, she couldn't find shoes in Europe. They had gone to Rome from Madrid. Frustrated, unable to get any sort of fit, swearing she must have been one of Cinderella's sisters in a previous incarnation, she went shopping for a hat.

The one she and her husband decided looked most Roman was a fuzzy blue felt with a veil. She'd never seen a hat shaped like it. Almost as square as a mortarboard but with a three inch deep brim, each point becoming a triangle jutting off the sides, front, and back of her head. It was one of her most successful hats. She kept it for years, long after she quit wearing hats at all.

How to darn a sock:

Her father had been away from home in the army during World War II. A large man, balding, graying, he was comfortable with his rank of colonel, accustomed to its privileges. For five years he had been looked after by personal orderlies, had careened about army posts in jeeps, handled every sort of gun, commanded battalions. Removed from the world of women he had learned, he said, how to deal with trivial domestic problems such as holes in his socks.

She was his daughter, thirteen, eager to learn. It didn't matter to her whether he was dressed in full uniform with silver eagles flapping on his shoulders or sitting around the house in old khakis, his big toe poking through one of his mismatched socks. The war was over; her father had returned. She would remember whatever he chose to tell her.

"Well now." He propped his feet beside her on the leather

hassock which seemed to be his property since he'd come back. "To darn a sock, you sew it, and sew it, and sew it. Then you cut the hole off." He looked at her expectantly.

Spring back, fall forward:

It seemed to make sense.

"No! No!" They told her. "You've got it backward. It's spring forward, fall back. That's the way it goes. Everybody in the United States resets their clocks by that saw."

She crossed the international dateline on the day the time changed in the U.S. and was comforted by the thought that time was an arbitrary notion largely devised by primitive navigators and farmers. Her own confusion would probably clear when she returned to her own country.

What to do when you're eighty:

"To operate the Scentoroma, remove the wafer from its plastic cover and insert it in the sunken slot in front of the machine. In a few moments, the Scentoroma will begin to operate. The room will be filled with the scent of your choice; New England Bayberry, Blooming Tearoses, or Baking Chocolate."

The colonel mused in front of the shop window. He vastly preferred the smells of dogs, onions frying, and horseshit. He couldn't imagine that anyone else would have approved of a roomful of any of those, not even his wife when she was alive and feeling particularly indulgent. In fact, he reflected as he strolled along, he couldn't imagine he'd like a roomful of his favorites. What was the necessity of the damned thing at all?

He called his daughter, "You ever want a Scentoroma?"

"Papa, where are you?"

"I'm out at the shopping mall."

"Well, I don't want a . . . a whatever."

"You didn't want the Beautiful Noise Machine, and I gave

you one anyway. Now you play it all the time. I hear it in the background. Sounds like rain."

"Ok, but I don't want a — "

"Don't worry." He hung the phone back on its hook and stood in the booth a moment, one hand resting on the receiver. There were, he decided, other things to do than buying foolish toys for his grown child. He called her again.

"I'm going to England for the months of July and August. Let me have one of the children, the oldest, the one that's named after me."

"I'll come too."

"You don't trust me with my own grandson?"

"Papa, it's not that. I . . . I'd like to come along. I'd like to get away."

"I'm sorry. You can't. It's a men-only trip. I'm going to hire a driver and a car. We'll tour Wales. I always meant to do that."

He took all three grandchildren, one by one, to the places he'd been telling himself he'd go someday; to see the castles and coasts of Wales, to the champagne region of France, to Kyoto in Japan. Then he came home and played the Beautiful Noise Machine while swinging in the hammock he'd hung in his living room. "Waves on a Distant Shore" was his favorite tape. He left instructions with his daughter for it to be played at his funeral just as people were tiptoeing out right after the service.

Sign on the refrigerator door:

If the water heater blows up,
If the gas goes out,
If the pipes spring a leak and flood the house,
Call the plumber.
"I don't like plumbers."

For reasons she'd never quite understood, her husband often took things too seriously. Perhaps psychologists spent too much time probing for motivations. "It isn't necessary to like plumbers. Just call ours and go away. Let him do his work."

"The reason I don't like them is I can't trust them."

"You don't know this man. The only reason you could possibly distrust him is you also don't know how to fix faulty water heaters, leaky pipes — "

"That's idiotic!" He folded up the newspaper he'd been reading.

"You're the one in charge of getting people to accept their own idiocies." It was, she felt, a fairly mild statement.

He didn't seem to think so. Whap! Whap! Whap! He hit the kitchen chair seat next to him at the table with the folded paper. "Why should that cure me of mine?"

"You mean it doesn't? All this time. . . . How long have we been married? Fifteen, sixteen years?" It was better, at times, to appear vague, to let him state the certainties.

"Sixteen. And, to answer your question. No. Curing other people doesn't necessarily cure me. That's why I'm so good at helping people in — "

"Look, some day I'll be gone and you'll need the plumber. He's a large, beefy man. Awkward. He drops things and he's sort of messy but he's a good plumber." She found a red pencil and changed her instructions to: "Go to a bar and call the plumber."

Bulletin board sign:

Do not hold hands with a boy while on campus. Always wear white socks with loafers and saddle oxfords.

She went out and bought a pair of black socks, put them on with her loafers, and walked across the campus holding hands with a boy. Nothing happened. She was disappointed; so was the boy.

He made a sign for her, nine feet tall, four feet wide. Black paint on yellow cardboard announced: SEX IS EVERYTHING. By pushing her bed against it, she held the sign upright on the wall where the sorority housemother spotted it through an uncurtained window as she was walking in the front door. Troublemaker was the designation given the girl; of course she was asked to move out of the house. Both she and the boy were delighted. This happened in 1953 when troublemaking was in its infancy.

Twenty years after she married the boy, she advised her children to watch their grandfather if they really must learn how to be troublesome. Or the plumber. The plumber was a good runner-up.

To divorce and find another:

For consolation she read books called *Fare Thee Well* and *Goodbye Please. Making Last Waves* was the one she began writing but never sent off to any publisher. What did she have to say on this much pronounced upon subject? Only what most people knew: buy shares in tissue companies, large arguments make costly lawyers' fees, the world consists of couples married or not. In her unfinished book she added, "Do not attempt to part friends with your husband. Once he was your friend. Now he is not. Why should he be? And most of all, do not go around town announcing, 'We're still friends.' Such a declaration deprives people of a good fund of gossip."

Oh, it sounded so knowing, so snippy. She hated her subject, not her husband, her ex-husband who would, she sighed while sitting on the edge of her bed, have a couch in his office. So odd. Most psychiatrists had banished couches and he was only a psychologist. "Sex Is Everything," she wrote on three pages, one word per page. He'd taken up with "a young floozy," her father said, "a couch crawler." Another Woman, she wrote, one word per page again. And once more, "There Are Always Other Women, But Try to Find Another Man When You Need One." She threw her mostly blank book under the bed. There were escort services. No, she couldn't hire Another Man. There was time which would eventually soothe. How hateful to think of being soothed! Her grief was a kind of pride. For a while it had to do. Finally time did soothe anyway. She bought a new bed, a new couch. A new man appeared.

She was standing in line in an allergist's office thinking it was not supposed to happen that way. Hadn't she been told to start attending church, or join a hiking club, or something that would introduce her to a man with mutual interests. Instead they had mutual allergies — to house dust, to sagebrush, to peanut butter.

In two weeks they had decided to spend a week in New York together. Getting away from sagebrush, she told the boys.

"Getting away," she told her father.

How not to get stuck on sticky subjects:

"Do you really want to marry my daughter?" The colonel played for time. For reasons he didn't totally understand, he preferred his daughter's first husband. Probably he was used to him.

"Yes, I want to marry her. And I want you — "

"I have nothing to do with that sort of thing anymore. Once you give them away, you're done. Nobody ought to have to go on giving his daughter away." He opened his book on top of his knees.

"We could go fishing," said the younger man.

"Why?"

"Going fishing is a good thing for two men to do if they're going to be in the same family."

"All right," said the colonel. "Remember that I'm old though."

"You can still bait your own hook, I bet." The younger man went out to gather up the rods and creels reflecting that his bride-to-be knew her father well. She had advised him that he preferred action to argument.

65

How to open an art gallery:

A friend from New York wrote to her in Santa Fe, "If you have a gallery opening and give people too much to drink, they will lean against the pictures which will naturally fall off the walls. And you mustn't have ceramic pieces situated so forgetful guests can put cigarettes out in them. You'd think people wouldn't act so trashy but they will in a crowd. Keep the pots high or cover them with those clear acrylic boxes. Use small plastic champagne glasses. Make sure two or three on every tray are loosely attached to their stems. Guests will constantly spill champagne on themselves or someone else which will provide a good crowd thinner. Do not let your artist invite many of his friends. The majority of them will come for the booze only. They never buy pictures. What is worse, they don't know people who will buy pictures."

She finished reading the letter and left the house to open her gallery. The show featured an alcoholic Indian artist whose friends were mainly cowboy painters. They painted horses, cows, campfires, snow, and serene pictures of wild animals. Most of them had quit riding anybody's range a long time ago. They had paunches, and memories, and large bank accounts. Her new husband, a historian, listened to their tales for hours.

The Indian painted large splashy images of ghosts. Warrior ghosts, he called them. And he painted almost abstract Indians seated in Barcelona chairs, or wearing sunglasses, or dancing in discos while wearing a lot of fringed leather. He was smart and sad, and his work would soon be too expensive for her place. No matter how much she reassured him, the Indian remained painfully shy. He drank black coffee all night.

The cowboy painters murmured friendly insults to each other, were elaborately polite to everyone else, and bought five of the largest canvases. The Indian fascinated them.

After the opening was over, she still had a case of champagne left, but the mineral water was all gone. No one except the Indian smoked. All the gallery's ashtrays held strange ashy compositions where he'd stubbed out his cigarettes. Was it, she wondered vaguely, a new trend in openings, or was it simply a matter of eastern versus western geography?

How to avoid making an apple pie:

The intense psychologist called to ask how she made apple pie and she refused to tell him.

"It's a family secret," she said, "and you're no longer family."

"Don't be mean. You know your father is still my friend."

"I can't help who Papa runs around with."

"If I bring everything, the apples, flour, sugar, butter, cinnamon — "

"No. If you do that, I'll end up making the pie while you watch. That's one reason we're divorced. I was always acting while you watched."

"You may be right about that. I may be a voyeur at heart. Perhaps I should ask your father how to make apple pie."

"Go ahead if you want, but I already know his recipe. 'Put everything in a bowl. Stir it, and stir it, and stir it. Sprinkle some cinnamon on top, empty it in the garbage, then go out and buy an apple pie.' That's the sort of advice he usually gives on domestic matters."

"It's the effort he appreciates, isn't it?"

"I suppose so," she said. "He's always considered small futilities as practical jokes, little treacheries he might avoid now and then."

"You are like him."

"Maybe."

She hung up and went out for a walk. Turning a corner, she found herself on one of Santa Fe's main thoroughfares. As she passed a churchyard, she was struck by the colors of the apple trees. Two, covered with red leaves, had red apples; the third had leaves of a luminous orange and branches full of green

67

apples. She picked a green one. Biting into it, she decided her ex-husband was right in a way. She was like her father except he constantly invented ways to circumvent frustration while she instinctively participated in those that came her way before she ever learned how to deal with them. But neither she nor the colonel could always remember exactly how they escaped. She should make a list someday.

Cowboy Movie

LL THE COWBOYS are cheering John Wayne. They have their hats on, and I can't see too well. I lean forward to pat a large shoulder, "Could you remove your hat, please?"

"Certainly, ma'am."

The domino theory works. All down the row in front of me cowboys remove their hats. A hand touches my back.

"Ma'am, would you mind?" Now that I have asked, he can.

"Of course not." The dominoes fall behind me. Mine is a big straw hat with blue and orange silk flowers on the nod all over the brim. I bought it at a garage sale for two dollars. Somebody asked me, "Elise, what do you want that hat for?"

"To wear to the movies."

"Umm." Somebody else smiled. They knew about the cowboys. Saturday afternoon kiddie shows play at the Rex; Saturday nights westerns are on except for the last Saturday night in the month when you can see a musical. By that time the cowboys have either gambled or drunk up their pay. They don't fancy musicals much. Lots of people in town don't fancy westerns. They have the cowboys. They have the West. They used to have the Regal and the Ritz also. Since the Regal

69

burned down, rats have moved into the Ritz. Nobody fancies the rats, so the Rex has to take care of us all.

If you want to see a western, you have to put up with the cowboys. You have to learn to be a fast draw with a hat.

John Wayne shoots a Mexican out of the saddle who's wearing a large felt sombrero. Our Mexicans don't wear hats like that. None of them are here. They're back at the Bar S, the Double Z, etcetera looking at borrowed TVs because they're all wet — every last one of them — and might get picked up by the Border Patrol if they came to town.

"Why did he do that?" Since they like to explain things, I ask questions. Sometimes you can't hear the dialogue for the comments.

"He wants the land," says Rafe, the cowboy on my left. "Yeah," Howard, on my right says, "And the Meskin wants to keep it for his boss. Texas owns everything from the Rio Grande to the Red. But we'd made this treaty saying we was going to honor all the old Meskin claims. I guess John Wayne didn't know that." Howard, like everyone else in the state, had to study Texas history for a whole year in the eighth grade.

"Aww," Rafe drawls wonderfully, "He shot him 'cause he drawed on him."

The cowboy sitting behind me paws my shoulder again, "Please, ma'am, shut them boys up."

We all hush. The repercussions from such exchanges can be dangerous. Nobody totes a gun, but they do have bad fist fights in the lobby which upsets the manager. The cowboys don't mind. They bet on the fights. I stayed for one once. It was about how many chickens were on the picnic table in *The Virginian*. The manager only shows what he believes are the best westerns: *Stagecoach, Red River, High Noon*, things like that. *Red River* is my favorite. This is the second time I've seen it. The only part I don't like is the stampede. Nine thousand head is a lot of steers to stare at.

Sometimes while I'm watching them collect I think about

why I'm here. The cowboys, the ones who know me, call me "The Spy." They grin when they say it just to let me know they're joking, but it's a half-joke. I was in London working at a bookstore near the British Museum. Looking at a book of photographs of the American West — much too expensive, much too large — I conceived a great hunger for space. The layers of history I walked through everyday seemed too heavy. I wanted to go home, not to Kentucky, to the West.

Howard, seeing John Wayne hire cowboys for the Chisholm Trail drive, whispers, "Ten dollars a day. Wasn't much pay, was it?"

"For then it was more."

I'm the bookkeeper for the JO, a ranch belonging to an old friend. I hadn't seen Charlie since I was a child, still I wrote to him from London.

"Come on," he replied, "I'll find something for you to do." An airplane was my stagecoach. I landed in San Angelo. Charlie met me in his pickup and drove home, about one hundred miles southwest straight into nowhere as far as I could tell. Finally there was this excuse for a town and twenty miles from it, the ranch.

The first thing I decided was: I will not fall in love with a cowboy and stay out here. I'm lighting in this part of the world just for awhile. Charlie, a fine weathered old man, reminds me of Walter Brennan, just in looks, not in role — he's nobody's sidekick. A landowner can't be.

Now we're into the long drive up the Chisholm Trail to the Abilene stockyards. Every time a cloud of dust rises the cowboys cough. It's their way of applauding verisimilitude. Rafe has pulled his bandanna over his nose. Howard says, "Thank God we don't do it that way no more." Stampede time. Everybody's whistling and shouting, "Head 'em! Head 'em!"

I go out to the lobby to buy popcorn. Despite being in a small town, the Rex has an ample refreshment stand, fifteen kinds of candy bars, three different soda waters, coffee, some revolting looking hot dogs — I've never seen anybody eating

71

one — and an elaborate popcorn machine. The boy who fills my order looks like a weak version of Dustin Hoffman. I start to ask him what he's doing here now. *Little Big Man* comes on weeks later. Instead I munch popcorn. Everybody has begun to look like a western actor. I'm afraid almost to look in a mirror for fear I might see Joanne Dru, or Vera Miles, or Faye Dunaway.

When I go back I offer popcorn right and left. "No thank you, ma'am."

Most of them make thirty dollars a day minus social security, and they are proud.

I go home with Howard and Rafe. Howard's been saving his money and has bought a new truck. Although he's had it for seven months now, I still keep the window down a bit when I smoke. He insists that I go ahead and use the ashtray which is, I fear, tantamount to a declaration of love. That's why I never go anywhere alone with Howard. Actually I prefer Rafe. Howard is sensible and steady: he could be anybody's foreman. Rafe . . . well, Rafe looks like The Gambler in a western. Howard is the kind that takes you to eat ice cream after movies. Rafe, out of deference to me, asks for a glass of water, empties most of the water out, and fills the glass up with whiskey. Then he winks and passes it to me while Howard eats his ice-cream cone and pretends not to notice. I think wistfully of how I used to drink gin and tonic in London pubs from stemmed glasses with frosted sides while I sip Rafe's raw whiskey and pass it back to him. We are loitering outside a drive-in, a building as garish as a child's new toy, painted red, white, blue, and yellow — primary colors to appeal to primary appetites. Cups and plastic spoons litter the asphalt. Something, some unrecognizable sound, bawls out of the loudspeaker.

"It's a song," Howard says.

"About un-re-qui-ted love," Rafe adds.

He's the most dangerous sort of cowboy, a drifter. Howard looks over at him. "What kind?"

"'Bout when you love her, and she don't love you."

"Or she loves you, and you don't love her." I poke Rafe in the ribs. If he doesn't hush he's going to be walking twenty miles back to the ranch. I won't be able to come to his rescue either. Charlie has gone to San Angelo in the only other pickup I can drive. I really can't get involved in one of their crazy quarrels. Right now it's spring, round-up time. I have a lot of cow and calf counting to do. It's considered impolite to ask a man how many head of cattle he's got. Out here that's like asking somebody how much money he has in the bank. Because I'm the bookkeeper, I know; Charlie has plenty. I only hope they're all there.

Rafe passes the glass back. I shake my head and suggest we drive on home. That won't keep him from drinking all the way, but it will get me out of the sandwich filling position between the two of them.

"You going to keep that hat?" Howard asks.

"Why not?"

He grins. Howard has a wholesome grin. If you can imagine John Ireland with blonde hair and without a sliver of meanness, you can imagine Howard.

"You think it's funny looking?"

This time he laughs. Certainly it's funny looking. A lot of raggedy-looking flowers frazzling all over a big brim. It was someone's Sunday hat once. I'm sure it looks peculiar on me with my jeans, boots, and green silk western shirt with real mother-of-pearl buttons, also bought at the garage sale. I look, as the English would say, "tatty," which is okay with me. You can't wear a dress when you go to the movies with two cowboys. It excites them. They start treating you like a lady. If you just want to be friends, you have to dress like one of them or a variation of one of them.

The moon shines on us all the way back to the ranch. When we get to the big house where my rooms are, Rafe opens the door and falls out. Naturally I slide out on the passenger side, but I don't expect him to be standing there with arms wide open. Before Howard can get around the truck, Rafe, laughing at every footstep, carries me to the front porch.

I kick as hard as I can.

"Put her down!" Howard hollers.

"Looks like a bride," Rafe leers. "I'm taking her to the threshold, Howard. Just taking her to — "

I keep kicking. Howard pulls on Rafe's shoulder. He stumbles on the steps, and we both fall across the porch.

"Sorry. I'm — "

"You sure are sorry." Howard raises a fist.

"Aww. . . ." Rafe lurches to his feet.

"Howard, he's drunk."

Rafe slumps back down on the steps and shuts his eyes.

"I know that. I'm going to — "

"No, you're not. He can sleep it off right there. Now go on to the bunkhouse. I'm going in." A woman gets bossy in a hurry out here because she can depend on a number of rules. Cowboys don't hit women; they don't hit men when they're down. Drunk counts as down. The minute Howard drives out of the yard I walk over to Rafe and nudge him with the toe of my four-hundred-dollar handmade boots. Yep, light brown suede with Texas stars twinkling in dark brown eight-row stitching on the tops. Except for movies, jeans, a few shirts, a felt hat for winter and a straw for summer, there's nothing else to spend money on.

"Rafe?" I nudge him again. "Come on. I know you're not really drunk."

A hand clamps my ankle, so I stand there quietly like a hobbled horse.

"All I care is Howard thinks I am. I went to a lot of trouble. Now you tell me I'm a bad actor."

I shift my weight to my hobbled foot. "Let go, Rafe."

"If I do, will you sit down?"

"If you don't I'm going to kick you in the head with my free boot."

"I notice you don't go anywhere with anybody alone except Charlie. You sleeping with him?"

"Charlie is an old friend of my father's. If I tell him you even asked such a question, I'll be giving you severance pay tomorrow, and you only signed on last week." I lunge toward the door, but Rafe is cat-quick. He tackles me and carries me back with him, whooping all the time like a barroom villain.

"Why haven't you shouted for Emmaline yet?"

"I'm trying to take care of myself, you lout." Emmaline is Charlie's housekeeper, a lady about seventy who puts up with no nonsense. She takes care of rattlesnakes with rocks, is a dead shot with a varmint rifle, and can throw a frying pan more accurately than most men can throw a football.

"I want to talk to you." He holds on with one hand, bends over, and picks up my hat. "Here." He slaps it on my head. "You're not from here are you, Elise?"

"No. Everybody knows that."

"Well, I'm not either."

He sits down on the top step, and I sit down beside him. Rafe, somewhere between thirty and forty, is dark-haired, dark-eyed. No matter how sloppily he's dressed, he looks like he has on a frilled white shirt and black silk tie.

"Where did you think I was from?"

"Anywhere." Some cowboys drift in and out. Others stay around here all their lives. Some are on the run. We don't ask. Generally they don't tell.

"I'm from L. A. I'm a scout."

"For what?" I look at the moon and stars, hear the coyotes barking, and think of Apache ghosts listening to Rafe and laughing.

"I scout locations. I'm also the director of this movie . . . the one we're going to make here."

I look at the moon again. Is it the moon or is it a huge spot light? The coyotes yelp, or do they? Could that noise come from a sound track? Are those stars clever glitter fakes?

75

"We don't need any movies made here. Everybody is starring in his own part already."

"But I need you. I want you to play the lead." He leans back against a porch post looking as if he's just laid four aces on the top step.

I rest my chin on my knees and stare into the dark. "Charlie won't like it."

"Yes he will. He'll like seeing the ranch and everybody he knows — "

"Is he going to be in it?"

"No. He looks too much like Walter Brennan."

"I'm not going to be in it either."

"Why not?"

"I've got my own reasons."

"You don't have to make up your mind right away. I will ask you one favor though. Please don't talk to anybody but Charlie about the movie. It spooks people if they know one's going to be made. They get self-conscious, and the script isn't even finished yet."

"Would you mind telling me what it's about?"

"You mainly."

I walk across the porch and slam the door so hard I can hear the porch swing jiggling on its chains. Charlie keeps the booze in the kitchen in a cabinet next to the sink. Ordinarily I don't drink anything more than a few sips of whiskey. Emmaline watches me from a doorway while I pour myself a nice stiff scotch.

"It's that Rafe, ain't it?" Emmaline's gray hair flows over the back of her long red robe. In the daytime she screws her hair up in a fat knot and wears frowsy print dresses. Her night clothes are entirely different. Stately or voluptuous depending on her mood, they're made of silk, satin, velour, velvet. A cook in the daytime, a queen at night. At first I thought these gowns were for Charlie's enjoyment then I discovered he sees a woman in San Angelo every weekend. Emmaline's grandeur is entirely for her own satisfaction.

"He's after you?"

"In a way."

"There's something about him . . . I don't know. Something foreign."

That's the worst thing to be in this part of the country. Foreigners are different, therefore, unpredictable, therefore, untrustworthy. Don't turn your back on a stranger. Maybe he doesn't know the rules.

"We were all foreigners once."

"Not me, honey. I was raised in West Texas." Emmaline turns her back on me and clacks off to bed in her red satin high-heels.

I sit on my bedside wondering. What if you once expected someone to come along and tell you they wanted you to be in a movie, and when that finally happened you felt it was too late? Those fantasies you never act on hide out like old booby traps — wishes to catch the unwary, dubious destinies for the daydreamer. I wanted to see the West. I came West. I wanted to live with cowboys; I'm living with them. I forgot about wanting to be in a movie. I forgot that when I was fourteen. There's no time now to fly to Mexico for a facelift, no time to straighten my teeth and pigeon toes, to take elocution or acting lessons. I might have time to go to the My Delite Beauty Salon in town. But they would only do for me what they do for everyone else, turn me out looking like a haystack-head, back-combed, blown, and sprayed until I'd seem to be suspended from the sky by a cloud of hair. Bouffant is still a favorite word in West Texas beauty parlors. It's the only thing about the sixties anyone liked in this part of the world.

If Rafe wants me for anything, it'll have to be *cinéma vérité*. My hat lands on a bedpost, my boots fall in a corner, and I fall in bed, a good place to stay most of Sunday. Monday I have real work to do.

Counting cows is a simple matter to anyone who never had to sit on the top rail of a corral and do it. Charlie's are number branded which is supposed to make everything easier. But number 803's brand has partially disappeared under hide and hair, so Howard has to find 808 before I can mark the tally sheet.

"You mean that brockle-faced one, Elise?" Howard only knows animals by their markings, and I don't know his language. He drives a splotchy-faced cow past me. All the calves are in another pen bawling, the new steer calves with good reason. "Mountain oysters" is a term I'm not supposed to know, so I play dumb and suppress a desire to shout, "Balls!" How would my English friends understand a bunch of cowboys acting like nice nellies about castration?

Number 803 is now in the chute trying to kick out. Charlie crawls up on the fence beside me. He's in good spirits as usual on Monday mornings.

"Heard you were wrestling on the front porch Saturday night."

"I run out of things to do sometimes. Charlie, who has been keeping these records for you?"

"Whoever I can get. Why?"

"Sometimes there's a note. See. Here's number 101, and it says 'snakebit.' Is she dead?"

"Depends on where she was bit. If it was near the head she probably is. I think we lost that one. We'll need some replacements, need 'em every year. Cows step in holes, get stuck in ponds, break out of the fence and get run over, poison themselves eating green loco weed in the spring. Any kind of stupid thing that can happen will. At least I know what's most likely to happen, and if we have a rare accident now and then it gives us something new to talk about."

"If Rafe makes a movie out here you'll have something — "

"I been thinking on that."

Howard and another cowboy named Spades line up a new bunch in the chute. Every cow gets rebranded if needed, and each is given a shot for anaplasmosis, a disease drifting over from South Texas that can eventually kill a herd. Then they're let out to rejoin a group which will be sprayed. It's dirty, repetitious work, the kind never shown in movies. Hereford cows, a western landscape painter's favorite breed, originated in England. Docile in any pasture, they grow confused and silly when hemmed in small spaces. Those lovely rust and white bucolic blobs — painted hoof-deep in bluebonnets on Emmaline's kitchen calendar — turn contrary, wheel every way but the right one, cluster in corners, barge into each other, roll their eyes, thrash their tails, and in general, act demented. No one ropes anything all day though a lot of whips are popped on the ground, a lot of dust raised. Not a bit of what Charlie calls "bad language" is spoken, not even when a cow steps on somebody's boot. I've heard stronger curses on a grade school playground than I hear in the corral. Cursing is an oral art almost like storytelling — here it's reserved for leisure moments.

At sundown we quit. I haven't talked to Rafe all day. He's been one of the drivers bringing cattle to and from the corral, bossing the wetbacks, hovering around the edges. After supper he appears at the door.

"Come on in," says Charlie. He winks at me and adds, "Elise, did this boy tell you he was raised out here?"

I know immediately Rafe is going to get his way. He can shoot all the movies he wants. He can use Charlie's ranch, his corrals, cows, horse, pickup, house, cowboys, cook, and accountant. He'll be allowed to wreck the windmills, cut holes in the barn roof, set fires in haylofts, shoot the antelope, stage drownings in water troughs, turn pastures into landing strips. With Charlie's permission he will mess up the rhythm of ranch life, one dependent on the needs of beasts and traditions of men. And when he and his crew leave, nothing will be the same for a long time. They'll be replaying the movie for months. Since he was raised out here, Rafe can meddle with whatever is here, and he'll take his version of here with him in film cans to L. A., cut it, edit it, send it back. Charlie,

Emmaline, the cowboys, and everybody in town will go to see Rafe's movie. I foresee a lot of fist fights in the lobby about how things really were. The manager will be miserable.

Rafe moves to the chair across from Charlie's by the fireplace. I nod and exit.

"Hey Elise, wait. Charlie and I are going to sign a contract and — "

"Sorry, I've got to be going."

"Where?"

"None of your business." Since I've learned who the real spy is, it has become important to me to keep my moves secret. More than that, I really don't want to witness a contract signing.

When I run out I almost run into Howard leaning against the porch post. So many people have slouched against it I don't know why that post hasn't fallen down.

"Thought I might knock on the door after awhile." Howard takes off his hat, a sign he's going to be serious. "What's Rafe doing in there with Charlie?"

"I don't know. Some kind of business."

"I come to ask you to the dance next Saturday." Rafe lets the screen door slam behind him — even if he hadn't I would have felt his presence. There's a sort of aura surrounding him, one compounded of shrewdness, power, and sex appeal.

Howard, innocent, hard-working, and good, doesn't stand a chance beside him.

"I'll let you know tomorrow, Howard."

"All right. It's just a country dance. There's one after round-up every year. Thought you might like to go." He shoves his hat back on, studies Rafe a minute, and walks off toward the bunkhouse.

The moon is rising, doing its tricks, casting cloud shadows on the prairie, casting rays on us. The slats on the swing repeat themselves on the porch floor. In the living room an open newspaper screens Charlie. He falls asleep in a paper cave every night. If Emmaline doesn't wake him and help him pull his boots off, he'll sleep like that till dawn.

"Now what?" I quit tracing a star in the dust with my boot toe and face Rafe.

"You going to that dance with him?"

"Why do you care?"

"Just wondering . . . thinking about the script."

"Rafe, I'm not your lead. Find yourself a real actress. I suggest Emmaline. She can play the gutsy western woman with a golden heart. Have you ever seen her dressed for bed? She's a combination Barbara Stanwyck-Mae West."

"I'd rather see you."

"Led myself right into that one."

"Look, all I want to do is make this movie."

"Who's the male lead?"

"There're two . . . me and Howard although he doesn't know it yet."

"Don't you have any kind of script?"

"The writers get here tomorrow. I'll tell them part of the story and they'll finish it. Then I'll probably have to change that. A lot is improvised. We isolate ourselves, live together, and see what happens."

"So . . . instead of *Grand Hotel*, we get *Raunchy Rancho*."

"Something like that. I guess you've never seen my work, but it isn't porno if that's what's worrying you." Rafe sits down on the swing. The slats' pattern flickers back and forth on the floor like the loose end of a reel unwinding and rewinding.

"I hadn't thought of the pornographic angle. And you're right, I haven't seen your movies. Plenty of American films come to London. Somehow I missed most of them. Generally the French films interest me more."

Rafe smiled. "I thought they might." His boots scrape across the floor: the dizzying slat shadows stand still. "Please sit down. I miss having someone I can talk to."

I sit in the far corner of the swing with my knees under my

chin while Rafe tells me about growing up in West Texas. I begin to see him as a child staring at a sunset in a sky so dusty the clouds are magenta-colored. I imagine him leaving a small frame house before dawn to ride out after a herd of cattle with his father, then coming home to eat a huge egg-bacon-biscuit breakfast his mother has prepared. My images were all wrong. His father was a bootmaker. They lived in San Angelo, and his mother died when he was three. An aunt helped raise him. She was the one who gave him books, showed him sunsets, and took him to hear the symphony. (Yes, he said, there was one.) His father, who had been raised on a ranch, taught him how to rope, to ride, and to fight. He'd detested dust storms, loved rain, and without anyone telling him, had always known a greener world was available. "You've always lived in it."

"Any place can feel cramped no matter what the geography," I say laconically, for I find it necessary to keep my past to myself. I was beginning to know Rafe. If he knew me, what would he do with my little history? Distort it probably, magnify my wanderings into a relentless quest, change my whims to the neurotic outbursts of an unmarried woman, turn my loves and losses into grim ironic despairs when some were merely interludes, romanticize my southern family by making them into a collection of half-crazy eccentrics instead of understanding them as individuals with peculiarities.

"I have to get to bed, Rafe. Tomorrow they're bringing the goats in for shearing." I unfold my knees, slide off the swing.

"Wait." He catches my hand. "You haven't told me anything."

"I know." There's nothing else I want to do more, so I bend down and kiss him.

Dissolve to my bedroom. My hat still hangs on one bedpost. Rafe sees it, smiles, hangs his on the other. We help each other pull boots off. Rafe admires mine. "My father could have made those."

82

"Let's just say he did."

"Where are you going?"

"To the bathroom to perform an act never shown in the movies — " I pause at the door. "Have you ever seen anybody using contraceptives on the silver screen? Even furtively?"

"You don't take the pill?"

I shut the door. "I can't. It gives me terrible headaches."

"Are you going to undress in there too?"

"Which had you rather? Do you want me to walk out of here a bare-assed, bold-faced brazen woman, or do you want to seduce me while slowly popping open all these pearly buttons?" I stick my head out of the door. "Please make up your mind. I'm nervous."

"I don't know who's seducing who." Rafe is lying across the bed, his shirt already unbuttoned. Did I do that or did he?

"In that case I'll leave my clothes on." They aren't on long. Neither are Rafe's. Our vulnerable naked bodies are soon covering each other's. Rafe shares my bed until around 5 A.M. when he gives me a kiss, dresses, and returns to the bunkhouse. Just before closing my door he says, "See you tonight. We'll talk about the script." Even at this hour he manages a wink that's both loving and lewd.

I won't talk to him though. I don't want my life reshaped by someone else's fictions. It's mine to make up as I go along.

Late in the morning while everybody is still busy at the corral Emmaline drives me to town where I will catch a bus to San Angelo; from there I'll take several flights to Bowling Green. I've left three notes behind. One to Charlie said, "Sorry to run. The West overwhelmed me." To Howard I wrote, "You really are a good guy. I wish I could have stayed for the dance." To Rafe I explained, "You're the most likable villain I've ever met, but I have to write my own scripts."

The pickup window frames Emmaline's blue-flowered dress and worn face. Last night after supper I caught sight of her in a black peignoir with ostrich feathers furling bravely around her neck. She didn't ask a question all the way in. Now she rolls the window down, frowns at me standing by my suitcase, and says, "You sure you know what you're doing?"

"No. I'm never sure, but things were getting too complicated at the ranch."

"Looked kind of interesting to me — you, Howard, and Rafe. Charlie signing mysterious papers. I hope he ain't selling out."

"I don't believe he is. He's . . . he's expanding in a certain way."

She sticks one arm out the window and shakes my hand. "You come back and visit us sometime."

"All right, Emmaline. Take care. I'll be seeing you." And, of course, I did. I saw them all.

They appeared in the only western I've ever seen in London, something called *The Working Cowboy* which showed everything men do at the JO in documentary style. Before it was over I was nearly exhausted from branding, corralling, castrating, counting, dipping, dehorning, driving, doctoring, fencing, feeding, goat shearing (done by a team of six wetbacks), vaccinating. About the last five minutes they turned from work to play. There was Howard dancing glumly but vigorously with a pretty girl who might have been imported from San Angelo.

Rafe's film, made too close to home I suspect, was so zealously true to life it appeared *The Working Cowboy* nearly worked himself to an early death out of boredom or lack of choice. You would never have known that any of those men gambled, got drunk, had fist fights, ate ice-cream, bought new pickups, went to movies, or fell in love. Relieved that nobody kissed his horse, I was furious to see too much verisimilitude turned the characters I knew into unreal automatons. At first I was sad, ready to sit here on a foreign shore and weep for the West I'd lost. Eventually I got out of the humor. It was only Rafe's earnest movie that changed them for an hour or so. You can't really lose cowboys.

84

Letter to a Friend Far Away

IANE, things are not going at all well here. I came down to the office with the camera. After two months in Mexico I've gotten so used to carrying one I can't leave it at home. My third eye, my reality screen. Yes, I will take pictures of the office I said. What did I see? A pile of boards — old shingles, hand-wrought. Shining in the pecan trees high above browning grass and withered bushes, a new tin roof, unfinished. Nothing here to photograph but wreck and reconstruction. I've seen so much of that in Mexico the novelty's worn off so I left the camera in the car.

I walked in through the back kitchen door, open in June, one of our most air-conditioned months. My artistic landlady shouted, "Welcome!" over her air-conditioner's roar.

"Don't you want me to shut the door?" Remember, if you can way up there in New Hampshire, our Baked Alaska summers — cool inside, flaming out.

"Oh, no," she said. "I'm painting my studio." While I was gone she'd painted a dozen or so enormous pictures. Why must the walls be painted now? Other people's sequences confuse me.

"A show." She explained, "I'm having a show." I handed
her a tablecloth, green, white, maroon, color-fast — the
clerk said — bought in Puebla, Mexico, a place I've been
lately. "This is for picnics."

"Thank you. I think I'll use it for a shawl." How is it one's
original intentions get so warped? Think of that time I bought
an abstract painting and when I hung it at home the meaningless lines immediately became Portrait of Fu Manchu with
Bad Teeth. And the time you installed the big window in your
back sitting room because you wanted to watch the birds.
Then had to put a curtain up to prevent kamikaze flights.

I thought about that on my way to the porch. The office
building is a Victorian frame house. Somebody walled and
windowed the porch, gave it a door, stuck an art deco light
fixture in the ceiling. Five naked light bulbs — clear glass —
sway above my chaise longue. What do I do here? Mind my
own business. Thank God my father left me some to mind. I
don't have a phone. There is a typewriter. I write compelling
letters to stockbrokers, real-estate agents, etc. Behind me
there's another office where book designers work. Behind
them in the former back bedroom a graphic artist letters anything and draws a lot. The book designers have a Cuban flag
on their wall, not for sympathy, for love of design. I gave them
a hand-embroidered pillow case. The graphic artist got an
onyx heart, already cracked, from X — I have forgotten the
town's name. In X the sidewalks were paved with onyx. Small
boys stood behind high walls cutting stone with power saws,
without safety goggles, without gloves. Natives told me to be
careful of dogs in the streets. Everybody looked hungry.
Amidst the walls was an empty crumbling cathedral surrounded by a tall spiked fence. A disturbing town on a gray
day, full of incipient violence and three-hundred-year-
old ghosts — cardinals, grandees, overseers, stone-masons,
slaves.

I was with Monroe who ordered onyx candlesticks for his
shop. The shop is not yet built. I've known Monroe for almost

thirty years. He drinks. He's a little crazy. I'm wandering. Too much to tell.

Coming back here is the reverse of turning up in Madrid right after Franco's death when so many of the street names were changed. Here the names are the same, but the streets have changed. A block from the office all the buildings, all the trees have been blitzed so a new bank can be built. I can hardly remember what was there before.

One of the book designers is drawing maps showing the movements of African tribes. They will scarcely stand still long enough for the book to be published.

To return to X. I met a woman there who had twenty grandchildren. The youngest ten lived with her. One hip was permanently out-of-joint from child carrying. That's the way they manage the youngest — wrapped in a shawl, balanced on a hip. She did not seem to mourn her fate. Her life has moved in an undeviating line from childhood, puberty, court-ship, marriage, children, to grandchildren. Death and fiestas interrupt, naturally. No, it isn't simple, but it is organized. Yes, we're organized here, however, the organization is con-tinually disrupted. Possibilities for derangement are endless.

My wall calendar still says May when it's late June. I like the May picture, *A Bacchante,* a costume design by Leon Bakst of a plump woman dancing with a billowing piece of material. She's wearing a gauzy print fastened with jewels at the thighs. Her long black hair flows through another strip of material. How could it have been tied? In 1911 Leon Bakst was not very practical. Someday I will check to see if he got more practical.

My friend Monroe, the demi-alcoholic who ordered the onyx, is not very practical either. He used to be more so, then he got tired of pragmatism. He's now in a muddle. Being rich keeps him in servants; being drunk he forgets which ones he fires, so they all stay on. Though we never correct each other, I hit him — but not hard — when he goes too far, when he tells me things I don't want to know. Then he says, "Do it again." So I have to stop in order not to indulge his perversity.

There are a good many things I don't want to know these days. Here are some of them: (1) who anybody is sleeping with other than his/her legally wedded spouse; (2) why anyone got divorced; (3) how many people the gunman shot in the grocery, house, church; (4) what has happened to Horace's last client; (5) how hot it was in Wichita Falls yesterday.

Horace hides the morning paper from me because I salt the eggs with useless fears if I read of atrocities before breakfast.

As I said, things are not going well here. What would you do if you came home from a two-month vacation and your scales were missing? I looked under all the children's beds. They are now sixteen, nineteen and twenty-one and still hide things from me, a habit they must have picked up from Horace. April just returned from a college in California and poked a grass skirt under her bed. She's not going back out there. Then Allen called to say he has my scales under his bed at camp. He's the nature counselor and should be collecting items like butterflies, fossils, and arrowheads.

"Mother, I had to weigh a big raccoon. He was twenty-eight pounds minus the tow sack. Then the kids wanted to weigh Cleophus, the rooster, and the possum. His name is Adolph."

I will never put foot on those scales again. News of the youngest: Alicia's in Europe. Sold her clothes, sold old newspapers in order to go. Now she's wandering around Rome carrying a light suitcase. I gave her a camera and told her if she looked through the viewer the little square that framed the picture would, for an instant, collect the world. I find cameras soothing. Horace generally prefers that I leave mine at home. He sometimes fears I'll get over-enthused and slip inside his office to snap pictures of his clients. This is a fantasy he insists on. Most of the clients are criminals. In the years you knew him, Horace was a civil lawyer. Now he's taken up with criminals. Says it's more exciting. I hope a similar desire for excitement will not take Rodney out of his classroom and onto the stage, a logical step for a drama professor though not always a preferred one. Should he be tempted, try to turn him toward mountain climbing, or soaring, or some other essentially private danger.

That was the reason I was in Mexico — the danger. Somebody got sent to the pen in spite of Horace's excellent defense. The minute the cell door locked behind him he started sending evil messages. "You wife's going to come up missing." So Horace sent me to Oaxaca, to a sixteenth-century convent which served as a jail in the Juarez years. It is now a hotel. Historical information is relaxing to one who must spend nights in a strange bed. I had two bodyguards — Horace's idea. My room overlooked a patio with a fountain — burble-burble — and orange trees grouped around. The oranges were as green as the water in the fountain. Underneath the arches musicians played and sang for people eating lunch and supper. A good place to honeymoon or to hide out.

The bodyguards, Fernando and Miguel, slept outside my door. Fernando was short with a bandito mustache. Miguel was also short and rather skinny — too skinny to block a bullet we used to say. They went with me everywhere — to the market, to sit in the plaza and watch the people go by — I sat between the two of them, our backs to the bandstand — to Monte Alban, to Mitla, and to every museum. All my pictures from Oaxaca show either Fernando's or Miguel's profile in the foreground. It was odd. Because of those two several of the Oaxaqueños thought I was in some way kin to the presidential family. The questions on certain faces told me they were dangling from the furthermost limbs of a genealogical tree. The rest didn't bother their heads. They accepted the situation. I did not. As much as I liked Fernando and Miguel, I found their continual presence tedious and my continual absence questionable.

If I bargained in the market, they outdid me. Once I got a seller down from twenty-five to twenty pesos for a straw hat. Miguel put his hand on his shoulder holster and the price moved to ten.

"If you do that again, we will part company," I told him.

"But, Señora, it's too high."

"You're taking unfair advantage."

"Si, Señora."

The whole conversation went on in Spanish. Mine improved considerably as I had little to do in the evenings but read my dictionary.

As you have guessed by now, I had to leave. Made friends with some people from Connecticut. Told them I was being held against my will. Goth-thick. Lady imprisoned in a second-story tower. Hoisted my suitcase out the window, climbed down the ladder I'd bribed the gardener to leave in the patio. (We did learn something in that expensive boarding school.) My Connecticut friends took me to Puebla to stay with Monroe.

"For God's sake, Annabel! Come in!" That's what he said over the loudspeaker. It was comforting to be welcomed even by an amplified voice. He had a system. You buzzed, he answered. The steel garage door rolled up for the right people. His front door is used only for ceremonial occasions such as large cocktail parties. I'm giving you the following conversation entire so you can judge the quality of Monroe's muddle.

"Monroe, has it occurred to you that you live in an environment that resembles a pen on the outside?" We were drinking gin and tonic by his swimming pool where yellow hibiscus blossoms floated.

"But don't you feel safe here, Annabel?"

"Oh yes."

"Most everyone in Mexico who can afford it lives this way. Broken glass on top of the walls is also decorative. See how it catches the sun. Poorer people make do with watch dogs on their roofs. Functional use of flat roofs. Everyone needs privacy and protection. Enemies are easy to acquire here."

"Do you have some?"

"Of course. Oh, they are out there." He waved one hand

toward the wall. "Yesterday someone threw a mango at my houseboy."

"Maybe he has enemies."

"My enemies are his."

"Monroe, perhaps I'd better go home."

"Nonsense. Have another drink. You're safe inside houses here."

Most accidents happen in the home. Every night I crossed my fingers and pushed the rug against the door to keep paranoia from slithering under. The pope had come to Puebla. Why shouldn't I be happy there? Because I was not El Papa.

To take my mind off my troubles Monroe took me to X. At one point he decided someone was following. I had to scrooch down on the floor until he decided otherwise.

When we returned to Puebla, we went to see a woodcarver who carved animals for merry-go-rounds — elephants, swans, giraffes, horses. I bought an elegant horse, wood-colored, not painted, horse-colored, sorrel after Monroe rubbed him with twenty coats of wax. (He consoles himself by doing small tasks with his hands.) The horse was rearing on his hind legs, his mane flowing in a brisk wind. I looked again and saw a frightened animal shying at something, his own shadow maybe. I left him with Monroe.

"You can use him in your shop," I said. "I've talked to Horace again. He says it's all right for me to come home."

"What about his killer client?" Monroe doesn't believe in explanations yet he goes on demanding them.

"That's really rather sad. He killed himself."

"In jail?"

"They think he took an overdose of something. No one knows what yet. The autopsy isn't finished."

"Why doesn't Horace do something less dangerous?"

"He likes to face it head on."

Monroe drank bourbon and purified water when his chauffeur drove us to the airport in Mexico City. Waving one hand at the gray polluted sky he said, "Just breathing here is dangerous." Then he put his head on my lap and went to sleep while the chauffeur played war games in the traffic.

I flew home with twenty children carrying tennis rackets to a tournament, their coaches, and several young women going home to visit their mothers in San Antonio — they took their children with them and bade their husbands fervent goodbyes. Passion drenched the waiting room at 7:30 A.M. Each young woman was accompanied by a chaperone disguised as a smartly dressed aunt. There were also at least two men returning from a trip to Acapulco with their secretaries. One secretary's eyes were slightly crossed, however, she was as you might expect, all bosom, a cliche of voluptuousness. The children ran up and down the aisles, the beautiful Mexican mothers put on more lipstick, the tournament players sat still and hugged their rackets, the secretaries exposed their cleavages. Horace's secretary has one she covers up in the office. I do not know what else she covers up.

I looked out the window at the snow-covered volcanoes and wondered when they would erupt again. If they do the U.S. will get blamed for it. Why not? They think we're up to no good all the time.

While I was there Monroe opened the front door and gave me a party. Embassy people drove down from the city. The scientific attache told me we were currently being cursed for causing drought. We sprinkled the clouds around hurricanes' eyes with magic dust, they said. This dispersed them, kept the rain from falling on Mexico.

"Did we really do that?"

"Of course not. We made experiments once — far out over the Atlantic away from anyone's coast. But as soon as the eye began to expand, when it began to lose force, it gathered itself together again and moved to Texas, Corpus Christi, I think."

I choose to believe the scientific attache. I prefer to think the rain keeps on falling on the just and unjust alike, and there's nothing anyone can do about it.

This all sounds a bit addled. It's the heat. Roads are buck-ling, chickens are roasting on their roosts, people are keeling over. It's 114 degrees in Wichita Falls. I was forced to hear this on a car radio waiting next to me at a red light. There's no way to keep bad news out. Several days ago an old lady died at home in bed. She had the gas fire on. 111 degrees in her room, 105 degrees outside. (I found the paper that morning after Horace left.) How cold was she to keep a fire on? The final chill? Perhaps.

Today in the graphic artist's office I saw a sign printed in Bodoni bold:

For FUN or for MONEY
but not
for FREE

Now who is it meant for? There are also some new pictures of mournful cows, fat ones with black splotches. I understand very little of what goes on in there. I understand even less of what goes on in my own house. Last night when I pulled the bedspread back I caught a glimmer of a sun shining under our bed.

"Horace," I said, "it's one thing to send me and the camera off to Mexico, but this is something else."

"It's loaded. Don't touch it."

"Who is after you now?"

"The guy who overdosed has a brother. He was the one who was going to get you originally, I guess."

"But we don't have to sleep with a loaded gun."

"Revolver, Annabel. It's a revolver, a .22." You know how exacting he is.

"What's it doing on my side of the bed?"

"There's another one on my side, a .38." I told him we couldn't live like that. I told him anything could happen any day. He could get food poisoning and nearly die like I did in Oaxaca. He could have a heart attack, a plane might crash on the roof, he might get run over while crossing a street, or he could suffer a number of other mundane ends. I suggested he

93

go stay in Puebla with Monroe. They could indulge each other. I suggested he have a good long talk with his mother. I even suggested that the graphic artist could make him a sign: Criminals Will Be Dealt With Severely, or some other more potent warning of his choice. He said he thought he'd keep his mother out of it for her safety's sake, that he couldn't possibly run off to Mexico because he had to practice law in Texas, that signs were ineffectual, furthermore, he wanted me to call the burglar bars people tomorrow.

I must rush. Instead of calling the burglar bars people, I have called a moving company. A small truck will arrive in a few minutes carrying several pieces of furniture. Little is required to turn this office into a bed-sitter for me and whatever child happens to be at home. There's a kitchen here, as I mentioned, and a bath as well. I am aware that a camera and a calendar that says May in June are the flimsiest of protective devices, but I will not shoot at everything that squeaks in the night and I will not commence the day staring at the world through bars. Horace wants an excuse to have those guns on hand. Well he can have them. He can't have me too. I can't tell you what has truly happened to him, particularly when you remember him as an affable man. All I know is that his search for something more interesting and his desire to monkey with the dangerous have overwhelmed him. I'm departing before I get caught in the crossfire.

Being a lawyer's wife has taught me a bit about the necessity of evidence. I'd appreciate it if you'd keep this letter. I trust it will arrive though the mail, like everything else, has been undependable lately.

Love,
Annabel

94

Graffiti

TANDING on the Left Bank, looking across at the walls bordering the Seine, Susan saw graffiti made of huge swirling letters filled with scribbles in pinks, blues, greens. There were smaller scribbles all around. It wasn't the violent sort, not the blasts of black and red rage sprayed on walls in New York. This looked playful, more like silly insults. Following the loops and turns as carefully as possible, she couldn't find a French word. Theirs, painted on the main streets of Leon, Texas, had been quite clear, white on black, easy to read day or night.

What odd things drifted to mind when one was abroad. Distance charged perceptions, strengthened them. And maybe it was the mixture of everything — the old city, the different languages, the jumble of cultures in the Latin Quarter — that provoked peculiar bits of memory.

Susan came to Paris as often as possible. This year her daughter was studying there so she had time to wander with her or by herself. She went back to the Seine, she went to St. Denis to see the tombs of the French kings and queens, she took the train, then a taxi to Monet's garden at Giverny, often she rode the Metro. Everywhere she noticed the graffiti and began to think of the big wavy letters as a particular Parisian type. Pastel pink, yellow, green blue, it billowed on both banks of the river, ran down the Metro's walls, sloshed over concrete surrounding the Pompidou. Theirs had all been white . . . whitewash slapped on with old brooms on Leon's asphalt streets. Sonny Williams picked up everybody at her house in the center of the neighborhood. She'd thought it was the center of the world at the time. Poor Sonny Williams, dead of a heart attack at forty. At eighteen he'd been miserably in love with May Sandifer who called him "Fat Boy" to his face. But on street-painting nights May would sit next to him in his jeep. An old broom, stuck straw end up like a stiff pennant, protruded from a flag holder on the driver's side. The bucket of whitewash and three or four other worn brooms were stuffed behind the seats. His broom pennant and the jeep itself — it had a top but no doors — gave Sonny an air of pudgy strength and good humor.

She'd scrambled in the jeep with the rest of the girls, all of them reminding each other of the whitewash. And those that couldn't get in rode in old cars and pickups that followed. They must have looked like a movie version of small town life in the fifties. Happy boys and girls jumping into rattletraps. Everyone wanted to believe in that innocent little world, and it hardly existed. The people she'd known when she lived there had the most savage passions, some so painful she almost forgot adolescence until she had to endure her children's.

In one way, she'd had more freedom; Leon was a protective place. A policeman stopped the light at the intersections where the out-of-town team's bus would have to turn the next day. While it shone red above them, they painted their sign in large block letters filling in outlines with great swaths of white. On the worn asphalt their brooms scratched, BEAT THE BULLDOGS! SCALP THE INDIANS! or some other jeer meant to insult a visiting team. There were no cops to help out on country roads. They spread themselves on the shoulders and shouted warnings if they saw cars. Not many came up Five Mile Hill or through Caven's Gap. Sonny said they painted those signs for everybody in town to see. No. They painted them because it was something to do, because it was fairly dangerous, and because Sonny Williams was trying to show May Sandifer how brave he could be.

Susan, on her way back from a morning's shopping, surrounded by Moroccan restaurants, bistros, bookshops full of medical texts, a small grocery store and a chocolaterie full of the usual marvelous French absurdities — candy shaped like ducks, like starfish, like pigs — swung her packages and wondered if she'd really understood those signs at all. They were bound up with the rituals of football, the one game everybody knew. Hardly any of the boys who came along with Sonny Williams played. Smart town boys mostly. They grew up to be lawyers, doctors, journalists. Other town boys who made the team were much admired. So were the country boys. She'd had a terrible crush on one of them, wrote his name all over her book covers. Larry. Over and over again. Larry.

She pushed open the heavy glass door to her hotel. "Madame, you have another call." The Tunisian desk clerk was too interested in her phone calls. "Romance," he seemed to hint. "Oh, Madame, your lover, perhaps?" His eyes glowed. He gave her a large, open smile.

"Wait," he insisted, "I ring. You answer over there. Now no need to go upstair." He gestured toward the lobby phone on the wall by the elevator.

She stood by it dutifully, and when it rang nodded her thanks to the clerk who continued to lean over the desk.

"Yes?" It was Emile. From then on everything would be "No." She could almost hear herself sighing away a string of "Nos." No, she would not go to lunch today, to supper tonight, to lunch tomorrow. No, she could not join him for tea, nor would she and Lynn go with Emile and his daughter to Rouen. Finally, no, she could not possibly tell him anything more.

The clerk winced when she slammed the receiver down. "Oh, I'm regrette!" The phrase stumbled on her tongue. She often began in French and finished in English. The novelty of reversing the error made her laugh.

"I mean . . . I'm sorry."

She had agreed to speak English to him. He hadn't had enough practice, he'd said. Many Americans and British came to the hotel. The Tunisian wanted to keep his job through the winter. He was a student and married. Dark-haired, dark-eyed and plump, full of domestic bliss, she'd imagined, full of couscous Parisian.

Susan waved to him as she got in the tiny cage of the elevator. She would try to appear friendly even though the Tunisian had forgotten he was domesticated and asked her daughter to go dancing.

"I thought. . . . Isn't he married?"

"Oh, Mother! He's probably one of those men who's married when it suits him. Don't worry. I like Algerians better."

Lynn had been studying in Paris for a year and her mother found on seeing her again that she, though still immature enough to be naive often, was sophisticated at odd moments and for odd reasons. The desk clerk was harmless because she wasn't interested in him. She had no notions about what desk clerks should or shouldn't do. Sometimes Susan felt her daughter was more worldly than she was. Sometimes she also felt impossibly old around her. Sometimes, she knew, she was supposed to feel that way. After two semesters at the Alliance Francaise, Lynn now chattered insouciantly to Nigerian students she ran across in the Luxembourg Gardens or the *Boul' Mich'*, wanted to return to Greece, and thought a trip to Rumania would be fun. She was busy fitting pieces of her world together.

Susan pushed the key in her door and began the usual fight to make the lock work. It was so dark at the end of the narrow hall that a light bulb burned all the time in the ceiling, a true reversal of stingy custom in little French hotels. Down the hall opposite one of the tall Scandinavian men — two of them had been there all week — seemed to be having the same trouble. What was that on the wall next to her door? She gave the key another twist. Light from the window flowed out into the hall. Well it was nothing much, just a bit of a pencil scratch, the kind she saw often, one announcing, "I was here." Though never as thick or grotesque as the graffiti in New York, these scrawls splattered the city, often appearing on sections of walls that had long been marked *defense d' afficher*. Meaningless, the thoughtless doodles of children breaking rules, or were they signs others read easily like the ones left by hobos? There were some whose meaning Parisians understood easily: Le Pen. Nazi. Then a swastika was drawn in a circle. A right-wing politician, Lynn had told her. Many people in that neighborhood didn't want him elected. Susan put her sacks in a chair and pulled her shoes off. She would never, she feared, get accustomed to walking the miles per day that Parisians walked. Oh, the delight of falling on a bed!

The phone rang. No, she would not answer. It might be Lynn. Couldn't be. She was having lunch with a Canadian boy she'd met in Rome six months ago. So it was Emile again or one of Lynn's friends. The ring went on ten, eleven, twelve —

"No. No, Emile!"

"I'm coming over to get you."

"You don't know — "

"Yes, I do. Lynn gave us the number only. I called your mother for the name."

"You called her from Paris? She must have thought you were mad."

"She loved it. She sounded exactly as she used to."

"Well she isn't the same. Mother has a heart murmur, diabetes, arthritis, and is walking with a cane."

She couldn't let him think anything remained as it was, and

no doubt he was ready to do just that. What right had he to assume that thirty years could pass without anything changing?

"Oh, come on." She cautioned herself in the mirror. "Come on-n-n." Perhaps it was better he'd found out the name of the hotel. Now he could come and see her, look at his fifty-year-old college girlfriend and notice she had indeed changed. Had vanity kept her from seeing him? Was it the graying hair, the ten pounds she couldn't lose and had, at last, decided she'd have to carry? No. She wouldn't accuse herself of that. Time caught everyone one way or another. Emile had not spoken of the years since they had met but how like him not to. He had never used American cliches. He was simply delighted their daughters happened to have arrived in Paris to study the same year and had bumped into each other midst the tangle of nationalities attending the Alliance Francaise. For them to come to collect their children at approximately the same time was, he said, a small miracle. An arranged miracle, Susan decided, since the girls had become friends. The way she and Emile met wasn't important. She'd been sure she'd see him again. It was this same certainty that had kept her from sending him a wedding invitation so many years ago.

"If I send Emile an invitation, Mother, he'll come." That was what she'd said.

"But what if he does come?"

"I don't really want him here."

Of course she'd been in love with Emile even though she had refused him. He was exciting, troubled, troublesome. A wanderer, a womanizer, a brilliant law student, a bad friend. Undependable, he drank too much, disappeared frequently. He'd left her waiting too often. Now she let him wait.

Susan looked out the window where she and Lynn had discovered two giant butterflies in the process of metamorphosing while clinging to a cocoon. Slowly, slowly they unfurled wings which appeared to be made of dark green and purple silk. The two of them dangled on the tree, unimaginably exotic, live Christmas decorations, silk-scarf escapees from a magician's top hat, signs of a hidden natural world growing in the old city. For two days now they'd watched their secret show on the tree that grew out of a crack in the pavement in the tiny patio behind the hotel. A small miracle itself, that tree. It reached to the fourth floor.

And behind it, a rooftop rimmed with geraniums where at seven every morning four or five men and a woman wearing white coats met to chatter urgently about something. Susan couldn't guess what common need brought them together. Wisps of French floated through the tree's branches; hearing their voices, she knew it was time to get up. And across the way only a story taller, was a round window in a tower just built to contain a princess, a countess, a student. Surely someone lived there and looked out sometime. But she'd noticed only one sign of occupancy, a dark curtain falling across the window just at dusk.

Oh, she should go down and see Emile. It was mean to make him wait too long. The only Hungarian she'd ever known, he'd been a refugee in Texas after the 1956 uprising. Some people in Austin offered to sponsor him and help him get a job while he finished his degree at the university. She'd noticed him pacing back and forth under the trees opposite one of her classrooms. He seemed to be saying something. Lines? Was he memorizing lines? She went out and asked when the class was over. He'd looked at her blankly for a moment, his eyes painfully alert, questioning. By his worn white shirt and black trousers, she saw immediately that he was probably a foreigner.

"I practice English."

"Hello."

He copied her intonation exactly then offered his hand.

She shook it dubiously. It was not a custom she knew. Her father shook hands when he met other men, but her mother didn't offer her hand unless she was standing in a receiving line.

"Will you have a coffee?" he asked.

She would. She would have whatever Emile offered for the next two years. How could she know his minimal English concealed not only a rich past but a mercurial temperament as well? She was too young for Emile, much too young, yet after she'd been with him the boys her age were even younger. He had no car. They walked everywhere. With him she began to notice that her city was merely a provincial capitol and all that had been grand, or at least usual, became slightly shabby. unimportant, comic. The firemen's statue was a piece of nineteenth-century sentimentality too prominently displayed — until he pointed it out she'd never really seen it — and most of the buildings downtown were merely brick boxes. Well, he told her, provinciality was really a state of mind and they were free to become what they pleased. He mourned for Budapest one day, despised it the next. His undergraduate classes were infantile, he knew nothing about the capitalists' theories of modern economics. The history of the United States was fascinating, a study of what free men could do, they had murdered the Indians. So he swayed. She learned not to argue. He fell in love with other girls too easily; she refused to take much notice. Every time he swung back. Eventually — she thought it was because faithlessness surrounded her — she left him for a series of young men who, she realized later, had suffered for Emile's recurring disloyalties.

All of that, she told herself as the tiny elevator creaked down, was thirty years ago and it might as well have been a hundred.

"My dear." He took her hand as she walked out of the door. His felt the same as it had that hot afternoon in September and she told him so, for that moment was so instantly present in her mind.

"You are still as pretty as — "

"No, Emile, I won't be charmed. I was never a classic pretty girl. I may be interesting looking or attractive. . . . Pretty, no. But you — you have remained handsome."

She kept trying to see the refugee, the boy, and it was

useless. Emile was as old as she was. His hair had turned white early, his eyes remained as dark. His expression, which had always changed quickly, was good-humored at the moment. He was wearing well-tailored clothes: a lightweight jacket that appeared to have less than the usual number of buttons, a cream colored shirt, fawn trousers, brilliantly polished loafers.

"I see you became a capitalist, Emile."

"Ah, yes, an easy surrender. I live in Los Angeles now. I have become a design consultant. Doesn't that sound important? I am the one who arranges sets of offices or apartments, chooses colors and carpets, picks fabrics, sometimes buys pictures. I even decide how the numbers on the doors should look. The law failed to hold my interest. Now I design offices for law firms."

They had moved out to the sidewalk. He looked rapidly up and down the street. "Not so many cabs here. There is a place nearby. Come." He beckoned.

She shook her head, more at herself than at him, as they walked to the taxi stand.

"We are going to the Place des Vosges, to a wonderful restaurant I know nearby. You will be crazy about it."

He sounded so like he used to. The best things, the best people were wild, crazy, mad. He indulged in extremities, she'd told him and he'd said, no, he only preferred them.

"I can be away only for lunch. My daughter returns around three."

"Lynn is your chaperone? I know you are still married, Susan."

"I've planned to see her then. That's all. We are going somewhere together." How like Emile to make her feel she had to make excuses. She was immediately angry because she'd let herself be irritated.

"I am married also. My wife . . . she is not wild about Europe. Your husband?"

"He can't always get away. Louis is a doctor, a plastic surgeon. His patients are keeping him in Houston this year."

"Yes. I know. Lynn has told us about him. But your clients let you go?"

"People in my business are supposed to travel a lot."

"You are doing well? Lynn did not mention exactly — "

"Oh, yes." She laughed. "I see. You're wondering about the hotel. Melli said you always stayed at the Carillon. You could say I've become a reverse hotel snob. I prefer the small places to any of the grand ones. There are two butterflies emerging from a cocoon on a tall green tree outside our window. I can hear the staff of some institute or other talking in a roof garden next door, and there's a tower across the way with a round window where you know you will see something wonderful any minute."

"You are the same, always making a little world around you."

* * *

From the vermouth cassis to the lemon tart and raspberry sauce, Emile told her about his dissatisfaction with the law, his turn to the art school in Chicago — this time he sent himself by working as a carpenter part-time — marriage to a California woman, and his final move to Los Angeles. "The Hungarian pioneer." He smiled.

And what was the sad side of all that, Susan wondered. Behind the facades of success, no matter how elaborate, there were usually large crumbling spaces of misfortune and grief.

"You are very quiet." Emile looked at her over his cup.

"I was wondering what your sorrows were."

"Not many. I put them behind me once I decided I was some sort of artist instead of a lawyer. My parents died in the sixties. I was never allowed to go back to see them." He was drawing crosses on the tablecloth with his thumbnail. "That was one. And . . . I shouldn't tell you this, but you've always listened so well one ends by telling you everything. We wanted Melli. We also wanted a son. My wife could not have any more children past the first. She refused to adopt. It made a bad space between us. I had been adopted in a way by the

McClendons in Austin. Remember them? I had a little job as an apartment manager, but they were the ones who sent me to law school. Those people were good to me. I was crazy about them. I still am. And then, you could say I was adopted by the whole country, by America. Still Corrine would not let us get a boy. That was the first of it. One way or other the rest came . . . happened. Now we are divorcing." He finished rapidly. "I no longer care about a son. Isn't that strange? My wife used to tell me it was a dynastic urge I would get over. Perhaps she was correct."

"Emile, are you marrying again?"

"I'm not so sure yet." There was a trace of a familiar tomcat smile on his face. Provoking, yes, but how could he have gotten through his life so far without that self-possession. Susan took a deep breath and looked about the restaurant. She'd been so involved in Emile's account that she'd hardly glanced at the place. Huge barrel arches curved from one high ceiling to another in the L-shaped room. A tall glass vase of fresh flowers stood at the corner of the bar. No flowers were used on the tables. Emile said that meant they were serious about the food. And, indeed, they had been. Everything was carefully arranged. To the chef presentation was obviously important, and while this was true of many of the restaurants she went to, it was almost absurdly true here. The green beans were laid in an over-lapping fan pattern, the fish fillet was almost a fish again swimming in a sea of sauce. At one point she was relieved to see that the carrots, though miniature were still carrots. The lemon tart was straightforward enough. She finished her coffee.

"Would it be too American if I asked for another? The espresso is so good and the cups are so small."

"Oh, no." He signaled a waiter.

The man nodded almost imperceptibly.

She seldom got that nod. It was something that seemed to happen mainly between men.

"Why are you so quiet?" Emile asked.

"I don't know."

"Why were you unwilling to see me?"

Had she expected something like the death of his wife or a divorce and feared the emotional demands he might make? Was that it? Had she been fearful of her own reactions? Now since she'd seen him it was difficult to remember. Uncertain, she shrugged her shoulders slightly.

"Emile, do you know what I do now?"

"I think Lynn told Melli you had become a decorator." He leaned toward her deferentially. It was her turn.

"That's not it exactly. I do a bit of that on the side. I've become a shopkeeper. It's one of those ethnic types of stores. You've seen them — bolts of cloth from Africa, Mexican masks, retablos, toys. Jewelry from everywhere, clothes from Guatemala, India, China, rugs from Afghanistan. Exotic, but I couldn't be more bourgeois. I bargain with salesmen right in the middle of the room if no one's around and sometimes we go right on if customers are there. My husband says I run the shop like a Middle Eastern bazaar — lots of variety, lots of color. I suppose Lynn told you she has two brothers. One has decided to become a doctor. The other is just finishing a degree in Latin-American studies."

"And your . . . your unhappinesses?"

"I've lost my father. He died five years ago. The worst was losing my sister. Evelyn. You remember her? The beauty in the family — tall, red-headed, flaming red. When she was thirty-four, she vanished. Just vanished, left a husband, three little children. We've never known what happened to her. The police say she may have been murdered. We don't know."

"She left no . . . no note or — ?"

"Nothing. That was the hardest part, whether she decided to run away or someone took her, she vanished entirely. I guess we wanted some scrap to cling to, something to surmise about."

"My dear. I am so sorry."

"Well . . . Yes. Thank you, Emile. It happened almost fourteen years ago. It's a real sorrow but an old one."

She pulled the heavy napkin across her lap and crumpled it on the table.

He shook his head as if he were denying some thought. "I am glad to see you here, to meet you in Paris. You will let me see you again, I hope. We could take our daughters out together for supper one night or we might all go by car to Chartres sometime this week."

"Yes. I'd like that. I always like to go to Chartres."

He put his right hand lightly over her left. "Come, let's walk around the Place des Vosges a bit. Victor Hugo's house is near this restaurant. Did you know?"

"No." She smiled. How like Emile to know where Hugo had lived.

"He did not die until he was eighty-three. In his house was his wife. Around the corner, his mistress. I think he died on his way to see the mistress."

"Incorrigible, wasn't he!" Susan laughed. He was still a charming man, yet all her old feelings about him, all the jolting passions his name could evoke, were gone. There was simply a certain pleasure in knowing Emile. While he paid the check, she sat opposite him quietly swirling a sugar cube, writing S over and over on the bottom of her small cup.

Songs People Sing When They're Alone

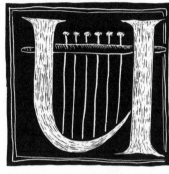

UPSTAIRS in his apartment I hear my friend Hapsell singing one of those songs everybody knows.

> She was pore but she was honest,
> A victim of a rich man's whim,
> Till she met a southern gentleman
> And she had a chile by him.
>
> Now he's in the legislature
> A-making laws for all mankind
> While she walks the streets of Austin
> Selling grapes from her grapevine.

Like everybody else, he changes the name of the city, makes it his own state capitol — fitting, especially fitting since we live only five blocks away from that heap of pink granite. I don't know why Hapsell sings this song so often. I get to hear it several times a week and I'm aware it has nothing to do with his life or any of his loves. Maybe that's why he enjoys it. Sinful sex, including old-fashioned repercussions, might be more interesting than the regular falls into bed he takes.

In the late afternoons when he's full of Teutonic sadness Herr Strook, the only other apartment dweller here, plays a scratchy record of Dietrich singing "Lili Marlene." He can't stand references to World War II which drove him out of Germany, but World War I, horrible as it was, is far enough away for romanticism.

Our landlady Mrs. Gaither, sweeping off her front walk mutters, "Da-ta-ta-da-ta, da-ta-ta-da-ta," goes in to hang up the broom and spills out,

> K-K-K-Katy, beautiful Katy,
> You're the only one that I adore.
> When the m-moon shines
> Over the cowshed,
> I'll be waiting by the k-k-k-kitchen door.

The lack of cowsheds, moonshine, or stuttering suitor, or the fact that the Perma Green Lawns Inc. truck has just arrived to spray her grass with some incredible chemical mixture which will probably wash off the lawn to the gutters down the hill to the lake to poison fish and man alike does not disturb her bucolic dream of younger simpler times. She is also fond of what she believes is a naughty song,

> There's a bar round the corner
> Where the gang used to go
> To see Queenie the cutie of the burlesque show.
> The thrill of the evening
> Is when out Queenie skips
> And the band plays the polka while she strips.
>
> Take it off! Take it off! (*She's inclined to get loud here.*)
> Calls a voice from the rear
> Take it off! Take it off!
> Soon that's all you can hear.
>
> But Queenie's a lady even in pantomime
> So she stops! And always just in time!

All these women are hovering in the air: Hapsell's victim turned prostitute, Herr Strook's bittersweet Lili Marlene, Mrs. Gaither's farm kitchen maid Katy and her ladylike stripper Queenie — fantasies of innocent maidens and bold sluts. I suspect they are used for reassurance of one kind or another: men will be rascals, maids will either marry or go into business.

What do I sing? A song of my own devising:

> Have you ever flown?
> Have you ever flew?
> And then come home
> Feeling blue?
>
> If so, tell me, tell me
> What do you do?
> When you've flown so high
> You come down blue.

I'm working on another verse that begins, "I've left a man who never loved me. . . ." But before I become the one-day wonder of country-and-western song writers, I want to stop and give credit to the little gal from Arkansas who stopped me in the Dallas-Fort Worth Airport and asked, "Have you ever flew?"

"Yes," I said to that pore lost chile, "I have flew." Holding onto the dead weight of my unused ski boots in one hand, I took her by the arm to a ticket counter and got her on course again. She was headed for Hot Springs. I was headed back to Austin from Santa Fe. You can pick up many a good line for a blues song while passing through an airport.

Hapsell's rattling the cocktail rock against my window. It's suspended by a cord attached to his terrace railing. Three taps mean, "Come up for a drink." Hapsell's telephone bill must be the lowest in town. People can call in, but he won't call out. It's a carefully treasured eccentricity. I've tried to catch him using my telephone — I've even pressed him to use it. He won't. He says, with all the prejudice of the true believer, that telephones are evil time-eaters.

"If people only sat down to write instead of phoning, a great many things that shouldn't be said wouldn't be said and a hell of a lot of unnecessary flap would be avoided."

Avoidance of flap plays a bit part in his life. It plays no part at all in mine as I find flap unavoidable. Hapsell assures me he could live happily without a telephone; however, his rich aunt had it installed since she can't live happily unless she can call him. She also pays the bill. The telephone is the only luxury she allows him. One of her favorite fallacies is poverty induces art. From time to time she makes unannounced visits to see if he's still doing poorly. If Herr Strook or I see her coming, we let Hapsell's phone ring three times and hang up. That's his signal to put on his holeyest clothes and switch the beer from the refrigerator to the toilet tank. Most of the day I'm at my place working — I own a craft shop in another part of town — so I miss nearly all of her raids.

When I go upstairs I carry a bottle of wine. Hapsell lives too close to the bone to afford booze for friends. Most of the time he doesn't sell enough sculpture to get through the year; he has to work part-time in a bakery. Between pounding stone and pounding dough, he makes it. We hug. Hapsell is a good person to hug even if you have to beware of his magnetic field. Like most sculptors he's got a powerful set of arms. He's no more than two inches taller than I am and on the lean side, though his chest is over-sized. Depending on his humor, he calls himself either Toulouse-Lautrec or Mr. Universe. Actually he doesn't vacillate a lot. He has a remarkably steady temperament and only two passions, stone and women. Somehow I've always escaped his tremendous attraction. I know it's there; I've seen the parade of women through his apartment. Perhaps we live too close together, perhaps our four-year friendship is more important to us both than bed fellowship.

"You didn't stay gone. I thought you were off for a month. You told me you'd closed the shop all of January." He pours my wine for me, opens a beer for himself. We sit in chairs on either side of his fireplace. The large black marble toad which usually squats on the hearth is gone. Glowing cedar logs burn through the day's last gray light.

"Where did you get the wood?"

"Friend of mine has a country place with a lot of dead wood. You haven't answered me, Margaret. I was just beginning to get used to your jungle and now I guess I have to give it all back."

We look after each other's plants when either of us is out of town.

"There wasn't enough snow for skiing."

"You lie, you debbil."

"All right. I lie." I drink my wine and look at Hapsell's fire. Its flickering light throws out shadows met by others seeping in the windows. Pieces of unfinished sculpture, most of it abstract, lurk like ghosts by the terrace doors. Stone juts into air, curves into itself. The huge room, generally a cheerful place, becomes as we sit there in the last light a perfect setting for an axe murder. I fear the black marble toad has crept out of hiding and will come sit on my lap.

"I'm sorry . . . whatever it was," Hapsell says in a kindly tone.

I break down, have a good boo-hoo right there in his beer. The arm he's got round me is also holding onto a can of Pearl. I don't like crying in front of other people: it's humiliating. It's more humiliating when you're crying over a lost lover and Don Juan is comforting you. In the midst of my tears I realize Hapsell is doing right now as many another man has probably done for his languishing ladies.

"I don't know why I'm bawling. I knew I was getting into . . . out of, a candy box. Sudden flights, secret meetings, remote exotic places. For years everything was so deliciously false."

"Margaret, you smart-ass, you ought to know by now knowing doesn't help."

I dry my tears on my sleeve, blow my nose on a dirty old handkerchief he's found somewhere, and get my back up.

113

"Hapsell, what do you suppose all those women do when you leave them?"

"Do? I expect they go find somebody else or somebody else finds them. I don't harm anyone for life. You exaggerate my effect. Anyway, we're not talking about them, we're talking about you. You said you left Henry."

"What does that matter? I wanted to stay. I'm convinced he's one of the few men in the entire world I could ever love. I'm mad about Santa Fe. I even like his art gallery and I don't usually like art galleries."

"You know what you've got, don't you? A bad case of the romantic jim-jams. Listen to yourself, 'one of the few men in the entire world I could ever love.' Think of all the men in the world! You know better — "

"Hapsell, you just said knowing doesn't help." He went back to his chair stopping to poke the fire on the way. He gave the logs a hard shove as if he was angry and taking his anger out on inanimate objects. After a few more pokes he left the fire alone and settled down. There was a lecturing look on his face.

"You expected too much."

"I didn't expect anything but disaster."

"Did you make it happen?"

"In a way. I invented somebody I wasn't. Henry liked the other person, the safe, unfaithful wife. When I told him Dillard and I had been divorced for four years, he couldn't put up with the single woman. I couldn't put up with the invention any longer. It was a ridiculous idea in the first place, claiming I was married still. I will say I didn't know — when Henry and I first met I didn't expect — "

"I was there."

"Yes, you were. You and Bea."

Four years ago Hapsell's aunt gave him money for a new suit so he'd be outfitted correctly for her daughter's wedding. Instead of going downtown and buying a suit, he went to the Goodwill store and selected a ten-dollar number that, when the cuffs were taken up, fit him beautifully. By using the suit money and putting in some overtime at the bakery, he was able to go skiing in New Mexico with Bea, his girl at the time. They took me along because I was just divorced and begging for distraction.

Hapsell sticks his elbow on the chair's arm, settles his chin in his palm, and leans forward, "As I seem to remember, Bea and I didn't see a whole lot of you after you met Henry."

"That's right. How could I know it would last? I fell in love with the man too easily. Naturally I told him I was married." I don't tell Hapsell everything. There's no reason I should, but what I withhold rankles most. I lied to Henry to protect myself, to make him think I wasn't truly available. Why? (I can see myself twisting the wedding ring I was still wearing.) Well, if Henry thought I was married, he wouldn't have to choose me. Since he didn't have to commit himself, there was no way I could be disappointed. It was an odd way to think about things. Why should I hope to escape disappointment? Everybody else has to deal with it when it comes along. I guess . . . right after a divorce . . . I guess I thought I'd had my share. No one ever gets to make such decisions, but I must have believed I could try.

As if he'd heard my faltering thoughts, Hapsell says, "Margaret, your mind is baroque."

"Yes. I mean . . . I know I shouldn't have gone on lying to the man for four years. On the other hand, there were times I didn't have to invent much. After all Dillard and I were unhappily married for nine years. I had such a wealth of bad husband stories."

"I'd like to know why you're so stuck on Henry."

"Why is anybody stuck on the person they can't have? Why does A love B who loves C? Is it the mystery? The lack of reciprocation? I mean . . . there are grown men and women who seem to make a practice of falling in love with people who refuse to return the passion."

"Yeah." Hapsell regards me.

I regard Hapsell. And, with an awful fascination, I watch it happening like the first well-known stages of a disease, a bad cold you know you're coming down with but won't admit to at first. Sneezes, runny nose, and by the time you realize what's hit, you're in bed with a box of Kleenex, a jar of Mentholatum, and a bottle of Bayer's. Choose your own brands: these happen to be my dependables. Hapsell didn't have such panaceas in mind. A box of Kleenex has no appeal for him. In the middle of being my friendly counselor, he has evidently decided the quickest cure for lovesickness can be found with the nearest available lover, a decision frequently made by others — two of my friends married their comforters. But how can you tell when one of these repetitions will bounce up on your own roulette wheel? I felt a silent current shifting, pulling us together.

I don't say no. I don't say anything. I grab my wine bottle and the nearest pot plant, a large red-leaved croton, and hug it to me. Strange feeling, embracing a big cold clay pot instead of the warm body coming toward me. Peering through the long dark leaves, a civilized animal in a domestic jungle, I head for the door.

"Margaret, are you afraid of me?"

"I'm afraid of being ambushed on the rebound." It's difficult to get a door open while carrying a large pot plant and a wine bottle.

"Ok." Hapsell opens the door. An icy sensible wind rushes in and the current subsides. "I understand. I am your oldest, most understanding friend." He helps me carry the rest of my plants downstairs. In an excess of gratitude, I kiss him on the cheek.

I follow the cliffside walk up two stories. Mrs. Gaither lives on top in a Frenchified nineteenth-century brick-and-stone house while Herr Strook, Hapsell, and I are tucked in our apartments at various levels beneath. I'm taking myself to supper. It's better than sitting home brooding, and I like being in a restaurant that's not too full, not too noisy, listening to a background murmur of other people's voices interrupting my thoughts with fragments of theirs. Seated in my favorite small place, one which is advertised by the most discreet sign in Austin, I look up to see Allen, Monica's husband, leaning over my table. As she is not with him, I assume she won't have him back. And, as she is my best friend, I also assume she's still angry at him. Allen's beard has grown in the months since I've seen him. It makes his face look longer, his expression, already melancholy, is more doleful.

"I thought you'd gone to California to live with a cutie pie."

He joins me without waiting for an invitation. Before I can say one other word, he begins a long lament.

"My life was dull, Margaret. Even the students in my art classes fell into types; the housewife who always wanted to draw and never tried to before, the old lady who'd been painting flowers all her life, the uncertain homosexual who thought maybe some hidden talent would explain his problem, etcetera."

He stops long enough to order a steak and a carafe of wine which he insists I share.

"Ordinariness was sucking my forty-year-old soul dry. I ran off to California, not because I disliked Monica, but because I looked in the mirror one morning while shaving and wondered, 'Haven't I missed something?'" He stabs at his salad and begins putting great forkfuls of it in his mouth.

"You're going to get a stomach ache eating while you're mad."

Allen ignores me and goes on, "Affairs with other women are fine for about six weeks. Monica is the only woman I want to live with, but Craig Daughtery is living with her. She won't let me in the house. I'm living in my studio. She drops the children by to see me on weekends and she won't discuss anything with me except what time she's coming to pick them up." He gulps a whole glass of wine, pours us both another glass, and asks earnestly, "Why can't a man have an adventure and come home again?"

"You can't freeze everything and everybody and have them waiting till you get back, Allen. Time doesn't pat its feet for six weeks. Craig was around and Monica was angry. Availability is half the game. You ought to know." Drinking my wine, I keep waiting to hear sombre organ music that will release me from this soap opera, a signal that I can rise and go at least until same time, same station tomorrow. Staring at Allen, I half expect him to whisper one last obvious provocative line such as, "If Monica found us here together, her husband and her best friend. . . ."

But he doesn't because this show goes on. I suppose it can't be helped. When you begin to think in soap-opera terms, all of life slides that way.

"Allen, if you were dying of boredom here, what made you come back?"

"I told you. Monica is the only woman I want to live with. I've tried doing without her and I can but I don't want to."

"You make her sound like a habit — dope, or alcohol, or tobacco."

"She is. Marriage is. I'm addicted. I had to find that out. I went away with Jill. She wanted to think I was not just a middle-aged man hankering for something different. She wanted to think I was different, or she was, or we were. Most of the time she didn't want to think at all. She wasn't shallow; she was young."

"You're going to say all this to your old woman?"

"I knew you'd be on Monica's side."

"Of course I'm on her side. What I'm trying to tell you is that some things are simply better left unsaid. I know a little about this. Here, sitting before you, is the local expert on blabbermouths."

His eyes lost their bleak expression. He smiled slightly. "I don't think so. I've been doing all the talking."

I lifted a glass in his direction. "It's all right. I'll get even later."

"Do you think Monica's ever going to let me explain anything? I've tried driving by the house every hour of the day and night. When she's there or when Craig's there with her, she won't unlock the door." He leaned forward. "She won't unlock it when she's absolutely alone."

"How do you know she's alone?"

"She turns the music up. That's what she always does and there's one record she plays, Offenbach's "Gaité Parisien," over and over. Loud. Sounds like music for the whole chorus line of the Moulin Rouge. You know why she does it?"

I shook my head in an attempt to clear it of a vision of a crowd of can-can dancers kicking high and swishing their skirts under the live oak trees on Monica and Allen's suburban street.

"She wants to keep me dangling. She enjoys it."

"Why would you want to live with such a cruel creature?" I laughed. "That's really perverse of you, Allen."

"All right, Margaret. You've got a wicked tongue. I admit I was cruel myself. Maybe I'm getting what I deserve."

"Nobody ever seems to like it, do they?" We both smile and for dessert order something called Chocolate Intemperance because — I told him though I would not tell my troubles on top of his — we both needed it.

I drive my old Renault home. It's a car without aesthetic principles, one of great age, no beauty at all, and it sounds like it's run by an egg beater and two rubber bands. My understanding of the internal combustion engine is limited by an unwillingness to explore the subject. I have no desire to become one of those renaissance women who can dismantle an engine, shingle a roof, repair the plumbing, and make her own spaghetti noodles. Spaghetti makers, plumbers, construction workers, and mechanics need their jobs.

When I return to the apartment I find my plants waiting where Hapsell left them in a draggled clump. I hoist each pot to a windowsill, load the record player with a collection of Bach partitas, and while these are playing I water, prune, and sponge off leaves. There's a sprightly order to the partitas and a definite feeling of accomplishment in taking care of green plants. Having them around answers an ancient need, a sunken memory of thousands of years past when we finally raised ourselves on two feet to walk about the primeval jungle. I walk about my personal one, a city dweller ordering a miniature wilderness because I cannot control the larger one. I discover I've begun to hum to myself. I turn off Bach so I can hear the tune running through my head. *Have some Madeira, m'deah. It's ever so much better than beer. Ta, dum, dum, pah, dum, dum, m'deah.* It's Flander's and Swann's parody of an Edwardian seduction. How could Bach's partitas bring this on? Oh, the trash in my head! Snippets of nursery rhymes, advertising jingles, what I said, what Henry said, how I wish I hadn't said, this light's too bright, buy new bulbs, siren — ambulance or police? — music, Dietrich, Herr Strook's at it again, telephone. It couldn't be Henry. The only number I ever gave him is the shop's. I will not go over there to wait and listen for a phone to ring. He had plenty of time to join me on the snowy sidewalk that cold night I left his house and he did not. He stood in his doorway and watched me go.

"What's the weather like up there?" I hold the phone three inches away from my ear. Dillard could be in China and still come on too loud, and whether nearby or remote, his ESP has always been weak. When we were married he generally wanted to make love when I was in a bad humor; now he usually calls when I'm unhappy.

"It's lousy. Don't you have anything better to do than — "

"I'm making a film about turtles. Just got back from Galapagos. Very strange place. Lots of turtles. I'm on Isla Mujeres now, near Yucatan I think. Been underwater so long I'm starting to look like a fish. My eyes are poppy and my tail wobbles when I walk. How're you?"

"Dandy. I'm having a party."

120

"Anybody there I know?"

"No." He never liked Bach and he'd consider nine potted plants nobodies.

"Well, I'm getting ready to meet Ava Gardner and some people for supper."

Dillard can't help himself. Famous names have always meant too much to him: he drops them like Hansel and Gretel dropped bread crumbs. Because he's forever the man behind the camera, playing the honest reporter making documentaries, he's self-conscious about his obscurity. If there's a star within fifty miles of his working area, he'll follow. He's a man who feels cheated of fame, a questing beast, harmless to everyone but himself. Oh, he's not gauche. He doesn't fawn; he simply collects names, and like my young nephew who collects stamps, he's fondest of the biggest ones. Every time he calls to drop the latest, I say, as I do now, "That's good, Dillard. I hope it'll be the beginning of a long and beautiful friendship."

"Margaret, she's only going to be here for two more days."

"Well, you can never tell. By the way, what ever happened to that bear picture, the one you made when you went to Alaska?" That was four years ago, the year we were divorced, the same year I met Henry.

"Couldn't sell it. It's in a can on a shelf somewhere. I've got great backers for the turtles though. Good distribution, PBS. Maybe one of the networks will buy it. It's all wrapped up but the editing. Dolphins next. Hear that?"

"I can't hear anything but you."

"Wait."

I listen to a lot of snuffles and snorks. "What is it?"

"Dolphins, a tape of dolphins talking. I'll be filming them by the end of the month. Have you ever heard the song of the hump-backed whale? I never knew how noisy it was in the ocean. Oh God, I'm half-seas over. My name is writ underwater."

"What are you drinking?"

121

"Tequila. I'm drowning my turtles in tequila. What are you drinking?"

"Madeira. An after-dinner wine. It's sweet. You wouldn't like it. If I remember correctly, you don't like any of the sweet wines."

"You're sure having a quiet party."

"They're all in another room."

I insist on saying goodbye to Dillard, who wanted to play his dolphin tape again, and go to my bedroom to unpack ski clothes. Humming *Have some Madeira, m'deah!* I begin to hope this suggestive sweet wine song is some kind of compensation for climbing out of Henry's candy box. I'll take what I can get. This time it's a song.

The Warrior and The Maiden

VERY MORNING Tim Warren
stood at the window next to a
mass of purple bougainvillea
tumbling down a wall and
stared over orange tile roofs
at volcano, church, volcano,
the theatrical backdrop to
this life. Snow-dusted, the
cone of Popocatépetl rose
high above the mist. On top
of a grass-covered pyramid where ruins of four cultures lay
buried, the yellow baroque church of Nuestra Señora de los
Remédios gleamed in the sunlight. Next to it another volcano, Ixtaccíhuatl, slept beneath a ragged snow blanket.

No matter if he knew the legends behind their long names,
knew that Popocatépetl was also called "the warrior" and
Ixtaccíhuatl was called "the maiden," they were Popo and Ixta
to Tim as they had been for decades to every other American
and, he suspected, to most Mexicans. For Americans the
nicknames were an attempt to familiarize the incorrigible syl-
lables of a language they found too foreign. They weren't
Spanish names; they were pre-Hispanic, taken from one of the
old Indian languages. He couldn't remember which one; there
were many and he confused them easily.

Tim waited, drinking coffee while the mist around Popo

blossomed into a cloud, one that would inch up all morning like a man lifting an old-fashioned night shirt to expose himself in front of the houses in the faculty compound. Popo, the slow flasher. He was tired of the thought but couldn't see the teasing cloud any other way. He was tired of his own company and relieved that Sara stayed with him on weekends now. She'd been in Cholula for almost a year and had gone home twice, at Christmas break and at the end of the spring term. Last night she had complained he'd been away from the states too long.

"It's been two years or more since you went home, Tim. You can't know how people there feel about things even if you do have a personal reporter."

Every time she returned she brought books, magazines, newspapers. Otherwise he had to rely on the BBC news and airmail editions of U.S. magazines which sometimes trickled down to Cholula. The mail was as unreliable as the monetary system, more so really since they could depend on peso devaluation.

The magazines Sara had been carrying slipped out of her arms to the floor. She laughed and stacked the rest of the stuff on the dining table.

"You know what you remind me of? One of those ancient Chinese emperors waiting to get the news from the far corners of his empire."

"Did you get to Dallas? Fort Worth?"

"No. I just flew to Houston as usual. I had to spend some time with my family. I didn't go up to your part of the state at all. I did bring back some new tapes. Want to hear them?"

"If they're country western, put one on."

"You're the only professor I've ever known who liked country western."

"What am I supposed to like, classical?"

"But you do like Bach. Bach and country western. If you'd just act like a regular professor. . . . Sometimes I wonder why you keep on trying to be a redneck."

They had quarreled then, just after she'd gotten in from the airport in Mexico City. He'd offered to pick her up, but she said no, she could take the bus to Puebla and a cab to Cholula. There was no use in him driving over the mountains to Mexico — that was the way she said it, Mexico, like the natives did — and fighting the traffic all the way across town. That was Sara, so independent she was prissy sometimes. You had to go a long way to do anything for her. That wasn't what they quarreled about though. Not that, nor the music. He was jealous, he realized, and quickly hid it because he was ashamed to be jealous of Sara simply because she'd flown to Houston.

He'd lived in Mexico three years and gone back to the states only twice. Too far, too expensive, and though living was cheaper in Mexico than it was in the U.S., his university salary wouldn't stretch over a lot of plane trips to Texas, as well as expenses when he arrived. He wondered if American history professors were well paid anywhere.

There was something else, some other reason hovering in the back of his head, one that he could hardly acknowledge. Sometimes he didn't let himself go for fear he'd get too used to the states again. When he considered this, he knew it was ludicrous. Everything changed so fast there. Whole cities were laid low and built again, so nothing was recognizable. They had over-developed Austin, he'd read. Houston was a series of eruptions — it always had been, and now there were simply more enormous buildings rising from the coastal plain. Part of the Fort Worth stockyards, Sara told him, had somehow become a gigantic nightclub. Skyscrapers multiplied in Dallas. In pictures the old buildings in any city were so fully restored he could find neither past nor present; what had been captured in glass, in stone, in cornices, and carvings was, what Sara called, the conditional past perfect — how the buildings might have looked if they had been perfect.

At least in Mexico they didn't tear up the cities. Oh, they tore up the streets a lot in Mexico City and they tore down and replaced a few buildings there and in Puebla. In Cholula, little changed. The plaza was the plaza; the bars were the same bars; the tortilla factory kept turning out tortillas, and the churches. . . . Supposedly there was one for every day in the year. Anybody could see this wasn't so. He meant to count them and never did, probably because he was usually drinking when the impulse hit him. Well, nobody was going to replace any of those Catholic churches, and nothing much was going to change where he lived penned in with the rest of the faculty only a field away from the university. The administration might build a new wall if there was room for one more. They liked walls and guards.

He put the coffee cup down on the edge of a table already crowded with papers and dishes, then leaning forward, hands on the windowsill, he tried to erase volcano, church, volcano from view, a mental exercise performed each morning. What was he going to put there if he got rid of them? Nothing, nothing at all. Immediately he saw instead a vast shimmering plain where dust devils danced through scrubby brush and snakes wriggled around cactus. The horizon was so distant he gave up searching for it.

"Freaking son of a bitch!" He kicked the wall below the window and hurt his bare foot as he generally did. He had seen the same place, the empty desert of Coahuila just below Texas, that tiresome space everyone drove through on the way back. Three years ago his wife, Janice, the empty-headed blonde, had driven north in their car leaving him with a second-hand jeep, a German shepherd pup, two bottles of tequila, a double-bed mattress, and a note: "You can stay in this country if you want. I'm taking the boys and going home." She'd been in Cholula six weeks. Ever since she'd left he'd been seeing the desert mirages. Not long after she was gone he began to think Janice wasn't so empty-headed after all. She couldn't spell, she didn't read anything but romances, and she was so disinterested in politics she had to be reminded to vote. She had a talent for fundamentals though.

"Tim, like I told you, useful people get used." She was right. He'd used her to deal with everything — groceries, laundry, house repairs, children. When she left he was relieved and somewhat ashamed. He'd brushed off her frustrations. The children had been sick so often she worried about them having amoebas, and nothing ever worked quite right. The pressure on the stove's gas was too low. Their shower didn't deliver enough hot water. The man who brought the distilled water appeared irregularly. Periodically all the electricity went off. She had to drive ten miles into Puebla for groceries. The refrigerator was neither large nor cold enough. There was no washing machine.

When they were eating cold food late one night, Janice rattled an empty tin can across the table and said, "I never knew we were so dependent on water, electricity, and gas. My God! Without them I don't know how to make anything go. This is the most primitive place I've ever lived. You need . . . you know who you need here, Tim? You need somebody like my grandmother or yours, some woman who was brought up on a farm before there was any electricity, somebody who can pioneer. They would know how to cook over the fireplace, make their own soap, boil water for the whole family, all that stuff. We ought to send for one of those ladies. I wouldn't mind seeing my grandmother right now!"

All her complaints seemed to be petty housewife's irritants until he had to deal with them. Other Americans on the faculty helped him. But once the original problems were solved, others arose, so he learned he'd never really known how much support was required to keep just one person comfortable. Finally he also had to admit he hadn't wanted to know.

About the time he resigned himself to tending to domestic tasks, he quit missing Janice which he realized was also shameful. They had the boys in common and her usefulness. That was all. His guilt turned to sadness because he and Janice hadn't been able to make anything else. There was a futility about his marriage which haunted him, especially the first year she was gone. Then it faded. He signed the divorce papers and slept on the mattress on the floor — alone most of the time.

He did miss Tom and Chris. The dog they left behind grew up to keep him company. The tequila, he drank long ago. He had agreed to everything Janice wanted in the settlement — the children, the car. There was pitifully little property to divide.

After the first four months he bought a bed frame from a departing couple and had a carpenter in Cholula make him a bedstead. A friend took him to the antique market in Puebla. Carefully he put together a living-room dining-area which doubled as a workroom. The table was Spanish colonial, the chairs at both ends were new, made of leather and designed by someone in Mexico City. On the sides he'd used old park benches. The rest of the room was furnished in a style everyone called "late moving" — a couch and a chair from other people's collections which they sold before leaving Mexico. Tim put his cup down before going to the bedroom door.

Sara had covered her head with the sheet. It cut out some of the light. He moved to the bottom of the bed and saw she'd found the blanket he'd kicked off. Probably she had been sleeping cold. That happened whenever he left the bed. He turned away and went out as quietly as possible.

"Ludwig!" Tim shouted.

The dog who had been crouched at one of the gates to the overgrown back garden, ran to him.

"Hello, mongrel." He scratched his head, smoothed the rough back fur. Now, full grown, he was strangely marked — too much tan, too little black, just a ridge of it down his spine.

Everyone in the compound hated Ludwig, yet Tim remained fond of him. A natural watchdog, like most German shepherds, he was intensely loyal. When he was around, no one but Tim could come in the house or get in the jeep. Ludwig spent most of his time in the backyard, and since he'd learned to climb the brick wall he'd had to be chained. Tim wasted hours unwinding the chain from old rose bushes and magueys planted by former tenants of the house. At least twice a day he cursed the roses' thorns and the magueys which were nothing but thorns.

The screen door slapped behind him as he went inside. Eggs? Yes. It was Sunday. Sara preferred to cook her own later. He fried two eggs and ate them with a piece of untoasted bread while sitting cross-legged on the tile floor next to the heaped table where he'd left his coffee cup. He could have done something more elaborate — home fries, sausage, and toast maybe. His father had taught him to be a pretty good camp cook when they were on hunting trips. It was more fun then . . . a skillet over an open fire in the woods, in the deep pine forests of East Texas.

He glanced at a stack of graded exams and a pile of lecture notes. Sometimes he thought the only thing he really enjoyed about Mexico was his work. He liked teaching, liked the faces of his students when they learned about the American Revolution, the American Civil War, the American greed for western land that conquered Texas and California. He didn't say much about the War of 1847 when all of Puebla had watched Santa Anna's troops fire on the American soldiers camped in the plaza. Every semester he let them tell him about the gigantic monument in Mexico City which celebrated the expropriation of all American and British oil holdings in Mexico. He was polite about that although every time he saw the statue he was reminded of the equally gigantic one celebrating the heroes of the Alamo. His discipline had already taught him there were many ways of losing.

He shook his head to see if there was anything left of his Saturday night hangover. It had almost disappeared. Some of his friends were weekend drunks. When they woke up hung over, they drowned themselves in Bloody Marys. By stopping on Saturday night, he felt he saved himself a little, for what he wasn't exactly sure. Aware of a sort of foolish pride in his own habits, he clung to each one as if his survival demanded them.

"Tim, do you have to slam around so much? It's like living in the middle of a storm." Sara drifted past him in the direction of the kitchen.

"Oh God! I forgot. I let the damn kitchen door go, didn't I? I thought you liked to eat breakfast on Sunday morning."

"I do. I just don't like the sound effects."

"I saved half the coffee for you."

Standing in the doorway he watched her sit down at the small kitchen table, pour her coffee, and begin peeling an orange.

"This is the way Mexico smells to me — coffee, oranges, Delicados. Even if I don't smoke, I usually smell them," she said.

"There are other smells. That too-sweet goat's milk candy they sell in the market. Aggh! And the raw meat in the market."

"Get out of here, Tim Warren, and let me eat."

He retreated to the living room. Tall and blonde like Janice, she was smarter. They had an arrangement, one of those worked out by expatriates who happened to have arrived in the same country. As soon as she'd finished her Masters in Spanish, she would return to the states where she might have to teach in some barrio of San Antonio or L.A. Even the poor villages of Mexico that always looked pleasant from a distance were better places than L.A. At least the air was clear in the villages. Sara would definitely leave, and he, yes, he would stay.

"You could go back if you'd give up being a history professor," she always said.

"Or, if half the history profs in the U.S. died tomorrow."

"Oh, come on."

"I don't know how to be anything but a history professor."

"You could learn to be something else. I know a guy who

was an English prof and now he's in advertising. He swears he likes it better."

"I don't want anything better. I like teaching American history at the college level."

It was an argument they repeated so often that Sara insisted she could say his lines in her sleep, and he could say hers. Gradually she ignored his pessimism, one of the reasons he liked her. She also had the ability to keep her distance, another quality he admired. Janice had leaned on him when he allowed her to; Sara refused to lean. She seldom confided in him. When she needed something, she walked to Cholula to get it. He had to find her along the road if he could. When she wanted to go into Puebla, she took the bus or rode with somebody else.

"Your beast is growling at the door, Tim" she called. "I think he wants to come in. And he wants me to go away. I wish you'd teach him better manners."

He hauled Ludwig away from the door and clamped the ring on his collar to the chain.

Sara, watching him through the screen, shook her head. He looked up just in time to catch her. Sometimes in the middle of the simplest act he was conscious of her eyes on him, and it made him wonder if she felt anything for him past a certain fondness. They slept together, they went places together, they were friends. So far she admitted to nothing more, and neither did he.

"I was thinking about driving up Popo today. You want to go?"

"I thought we were going into Cholula to pick up the chairs the carpenter's repairing."

"Oh well. I've done without those chairs this long. People can sit on one of the benches another month or so."

"Adapting, aren't you?"

"Yes." He laughed. The elasticity of time in Mexico pleased him. Procrastination was acceptable, in fact it was ritualized.

No one, no one but foreigners came to parties or kept any sort of appointment on time. There was a built-in set of allowances one made. At the university all students were required to be on time while the faculty forgave each other for any tardiness and the president showed up when it suited him.

Sara smiled. "All right, let's go, but I don't want to take Ludwig along."

"He needs to get off the chain."

"I'm not going anywhere with that dog." Of course she wasn't, not Sara. She had insisted on her terms from the beginning, and he had agreed to them. They were reasonable and interfered with none of his freedoms. In the compound where everybody knew everybody else's business, they lived a discreet public life. On the weekends she came home with him, or he went over to her place. He'd rather go to hers. Somehow it was more like a real house with pictures, rugs, pottery, masks, plants.

"How do you do it?" he'd said the first time he walked into her living room and was struck by his own aridity. He knew some basic design facts — couch, coffee table, chair positions, which any idiot knew. Beyond that he had a hard time guessing what he'd like or what would look good.

"This place wasn't so hard to work with. You know the casitas come furnished. The refrigerator is permanently stuck in the living room. I guess it was installed by somebody who thought it belonged there. It doesn't matter really."

It delighted him that she could care and, at the same instant, not care how things looked. Later he realized it was one of his own traits.

"Would you help me with my house?"

"Of course. If you want."

He'd wanted Sara more than an interior decorator at the moment. He continued to want her. If she wasn't available he wanted her more. The ratio of his desire to her distance amused and appalled him. She refused to tell him the last two times before she went to Mexico City for a long weekend. She said she had research to do in one of the libraries there. That was any academic's excuse. He knew because he'd used it himself to get away from Janice when domesticity closed in. Had Sara taken up with someone else? He couldn't ask. She was only twenty-five, ten years younger than he was, and she had told him frequently that she thought jealousy was one of the more idiotic passions. Despite her pronouncements, he was irrationally — idiotically — jealous. He could, he imagined, litter the streets with bodies of Mexican men who had lusted after Sara. He had an army .45, one he'd smuggled into Mexico and kept in a drawer.

Behind him somewhere in the living room, Sara said, "I've decided you're one of those men who likes to live in his own squalor. The cobwebs are becoming architectural in here. They're making vaults in the corners. Have you noticed them at all?"

"What?" He threw a loaf of bread into a basket. To get a picnic together he found the bread, then opened the refrigerator and searched for anything else edible. "Come in here and help me find our lunch."

"Your cobwebs are works of art."

"You know I need a maid, but I can't afford one. Child support."

"Yes, you told me. Do you remember what else you said? I was impressed. There's a responsible parent, I thought."

"All right. I know. I said, 'They are my children.'" He couldn't imagine what his sons were like now. Seeing them only at Christmas at his parents' farm in East Texas, he found both of them so changed each time. Little boys, six and eight the last Christmas he was home, struggling to build a snowman, sitting quietly with him in a duck blind out on the lake in the mist, rolling together on the front lawn. The youngest, Tom, climbed in his lap to ask about the Caddo Indians. Probably too old to do that now. Probably he'd given up laps and Indians. Chris, the oldest, leading the farm's only horse back to the barn in the twilight. Glimpses . . . all he had.

They had made him tell about Mexico because they remembered nothing but the journey. He told them the good parts,
talked about the mountains, the unchanging village, the firecrackers at every fiesta, the sound of the balloon man's beck-
oning whistle in the plaza, the church bells that began every
day, and the brass band every town had to have for every
occasion.

He'd played the Pied Piper well. Both boys wanted to go
back with him. Their mother, ruling from Fort Worth, would
not hear of it. Perhaps she was right. What would he have
done with two small boys in Mexico? He wouldn't have a
chance to find out. Custody was Janice's privilege, and she
used it like a whip.

"Buenos dias." The guard, a fat man wearing dark glasses as
most of them did, dropped the chain at the gate which was the
last barrier before the road to Cholula or to Puebla in the
opposite direction.

The chain clinked when it hit the asphalt. Within the
compound were neat brick houses with green lawns such as
one might see in a crowded suburb in the states. Brick walls
divided yards; another one stood between the houses and du-
plexes that Sara called casitas, and one long curving wall drew
a wobbly line between the campus, a field, and the compound. Everybody lived in an irregular set of Chinese boxes.
To walk to class or to his office, he crawled over a ladder
propped against his back wall and crossed the field. Other
faculty members had ladders also. They waved when they saw
each other climbing over the top of the wall. Some days it
looked as if they were all abandoning a fort.

Sara spoke to the guard as they went out the gate. He
didn't. He knew all the ordinary greetings and farewells, how
to read road signs, to call for the check, to count, to ask for
everything he needed — food, drink, toilets, hotel rooms,
someone who spoke English. But that was the extent of his
Spanish. The language remained alien, for he had, half-
consciously, an almost magical belief that if he learned it he

134

would become one of them. Of course he wouldn't really. Whenever the idea surfaced he put it aside.

"Why couldn't you give the man a simple 'Buenos dias'? Some days I think you — I think you are the most stubborn person I've ever known!"

"Sara, let's don't have this argument again. I have a fundamental aversion to foreign languages like you have one to organic chemistry. I had to learn to read German and French in graduate school. That's enough."

"That's no excuse, not a real one." She turned and looked out the window beside her.

"It's going to have to do for now. Come on, Sara. It's Sunday. We don't have to improve ourselves on Sunday.. Come on." He smiled as he shifted the gears down. It was necessary to drive slowly.

People on foot lined the road to Cholula. Sunday was market day. Over at the corral where women hung their wash to dry on the crooked board fence during the week, riders now practiced calf-roping. He'd watched men do that in Texas when he was a boy. Why did it look so different in Mexico? The charro hats obviously. Perhaps they had to practice keeping them on while riding. Across from the corral rose the giant grass-covered Tepanapa pyramid with the yellow church on top, part of the scene he erased every morning. Behind the corral stood another smaller pyramid. He'd discovered it while climbing to the top of Tepanapa. They were everywhere. The old cultures never seemed to tire of repeating the volcano's shape. Since every square inch of soil had to be used, the Mexicans farmed the worn-away tops of the pyramids. Some weekends he searched freshly plowed corn rows around other towns nearby where pottery shards and fragments of obsidian arrowheads sprouted from the dirt like strange mutations of a past which an army of archeologists could never fully recapture. Though he could imagine American Revolutionary War skirmishes, Civil War battles, First World War trenches, the beach invasions of the

Second World War, and even the jungles of Southeast Asia, he had no patience with the rise and fall, the evasive driftings of Mayas, Olmecs, Toltecs, Aztecs. Oh, he knew the larger facts about the Spanish conquest. The road they were driving was called the Paseo de Cortes, a grand name for a dirt track, the same route, he was told, Cortes took over the mountains to invade the Aztec capital. But the whole interwoven Mexican past was hidden from him. Like the shards, it remained fragmented. It was all so old, so defeated. The various empires seemed so ephemeral.

He couldn't force himself to care if the French were defeated in Puebla on Cinco de Mayo or that the 1910 Revolution began on Diez y Seis de Septiembre. He did join other Americans celebrating the Fourth of July with barbeque and firecrackers. The parties, so far from the U.S., made him feel foolish. It was as if he belonged to neither country, as if the compound full of teachers from different countries — Germany, Spain, Turkey, Argentina, India even — was located in no-man's-land.

"Sometimes I think you like to hit the potholes." Sara laughed as she bounced in the seat next to him. She was in a better humor. "What are you doing on this street, trying to avoid the mercado? You know there's no avoiding every one of them. Sunday is the big day for these villages."

"I know." He swerved so he wouldn't hit a cart. Every other town would be a smaller version of Cholula — fewer tile-covered church roofs, fewer houses, smaller markets, just as many flies and skinny dogs. He'd learned to look out for rabid dogs. Everybody was afraid of them — every foreigner was — just as they all feared amoebic dysentery. The general fears of outsiders living in Mexico — dogs, dysentery, devaluation.

It was good to get out in the country to escape the narrow streets, get away from oppressive, blank white walls, continual stares. The natives stared insistently at any passing gringo. He and Sara were both blond-haired, and to make it worse, he was tall and blue-eyed while Sara was also blue-eyed and her

136

hair had been bleached almost white by the mountain sun. The conquistadors conquered? Maybe. In a third world country with terrible economic problems, he, an American, stayed because he needed the job Mexico could give him. He was a sort of academic wetback. But how many Mexicans wanted to teach American history? His students took it to satisfy requirements for advanced degrees at U.S. colleges, or said they did. Foolish of him to stay? Yes. There were many foolish jobs. His was no more so than the armed guard's at the gate.

"Could you turn here to the left? We could stop by Tonanzintla. It isn't far."

"You really like that church, don't you?"

"Santa María, yes."

It was a church the Spanish had let the Indians from the nearby villages decorate according to their own wishes. They made the cherubs flying down from the ceiling, surrounded by bunches of grapes and flowers, look like Indians. The first time he'd seen it, Tim thought it was the most exuberant church he'd ever been in. Near the cherubs were columns covered with protective angels wearing short skirts. The colors — brilliant reds, blues, greens, yellows — dizzied him. He usually went outside blinking his eyes, and the odd thing was he never got through seeing it. Looking at Santa María again, he saw parts he'd missed.

"Oh," Sara whispered, "there's a wedding." They were halfway down the aisle when she noticed. Slowly they edged over to one side. All the faces around the bride and groom were solemn. Indian faces, withdrawn, secret, concentrated on the mass. He had such perfunctory beliefs that at such times, in the midst of other people's ceremonies, he regretted his loss. He glanced up at the cherubs. Forever held, forever in motion, they were entirely joyful.

One of the old women wearing a blue shawl round her head twisted about to stare at them. There was usually one who did in any group. They made him self-conscious, but Sara only laughed about the stares and said he would be sorry when he went home because he'd never again get so much attention in his whole life.

He looked at her and saw tears running down her cheeks. "Do you cry at any wedding?"

"All of them. Come on. Let's go." She wiped her eyes with the back of her hand.

After they were back on the road, Sara said, "I didn't mean that about you trying to hit the potholes. You're a good driver actually."

"It's one of the few things I do well, and I'm not going to be able to do it much longer. I have to take the jeep up to the border . . . store it there or leave it with somebody. You know the law. Americans have to drive Mexican-made cars if they work here or foreign ones put together in Mexico."

"Why do you think that's a strange law?"

"There are stranger ones. I can't carry my .45 while every peasant who wants to carries a rifle."

"Illegally, Tim. Anyway, what would you do with a .45?"

"Protect myself."

"From what?"

"Everybody. Their legal system is no help. You know what happens if you stop to look after anyone who's been in a car wreck."

"You may be jailed as an accessory to the crime," Sara said as if it were a phrase that had been hard to memorize. "But, Tim," she sighed, "you know the answer to all of that."

"Yes. It's another country. But it's not so bad when you're around."

He did like getting out of the compound with Sara, especially when they could roam the countryside. It hadn't been used up by highways and railroads yet. The mountains, full of hidden streams, waterfalls, and strange birds, were easy to reach in his jeep. Sara was staring out the windshield with a determined look on her face. She had a feeling for the place, for all of Mexico, he didn't think he could ever have. Maybe knowing the language gave her some kind of loyalty.

Before them the valley widened. They drove by cactus fences. Tall purple and red wildflowers grew by the roadside. Not so far away were cornfields, trees, intertwined with an orange parasitic vine, little arroyos full of muddy water, foothills covered with more patches of corn. Nearer now but still looking like a stage backdrop, were Popo and Ixta. Lava rock from long-ago eruptions would be for sale higher up. Beside the road two woodcutters led burros carrying neatly tied bundles of sticks. They were walking along so quietly he regretted the jeep's noisy gears. He was an intruder; they belonged there searching out the forest for what little it could still provide. The woods in the mountains had been cut over too often and now it was forbidden to take any full-grown trees. How long had it been since he'd seen a real log? In Marshall, some time back. Christmas . . . two years ago, his father in a violent tantrum kicked one so hard the sparks flew. Later he apologized for "the Warren outburst." Their furniture and china suffered from it too; chairs were often knocked over and plates broken. Every now and then his mother simply bought new ones. There were a lot of mismatched plates around. Bad temper ran in the family, the easy excuse. Blame flaws on ancestral misbehavior, a perfect absolution when all the ancestors were dead. He hadn't forgotten his father's scenes. He complained shamelessly, cursed freely, but seldom lost his temper in public, not even in Mexico.

"Women, keepers of the external world," he said as Sara crawled back in the jeep with a sackful of pinecones.

"You mean men build roads and bridges, but they're not interested in baskets full of pinecones and other such flimsy decor."

"That's unfair. I never said — "

"I know." She smiled. "You're such a collection of contradictions. You like my place, have asked for my help, and when

I gather pinecones for your fire, you make some comment about how unimportant it all is."

"You don't get to read my mind, Sara. Remember? I didn't say anything you did was unimportant."

"Sorry. Every time I come here back from the states I'm . . . I get angry too easily. When I see the women in the villages particularly. . . . They bow their heads and go to church. After a while it really bothers me. I can never be totally comfortable in Mexico. I spend too much time comparing."

He started the jeep and they bounced on up the road. "Isn't it more historic and economic than political, Sara? Mexico, after all, inherited Spain's point of view about men and women."

"Well you could say that Spain inherited the Moors' and the Moors got theirs from somebody else, and where are you going to stop? We could keep on going into pre-history couldn't we?"

"Yes, but let's don't." He laughed quickly. "All right."

She wasn't finished. He could see she would return to her point. Sara wasn't one to accept precedence as an answer for anything which drove them to disagree frequently, for he sometimes found history comforting. That was the trouble; where he found explanations, she found excuses. His answers were often her questions. If it was true that you had to love someone to fight with them, he and Sara truly were lovers. They had fought so often in the year she'd been there. The worst time was soon after they started sleeping together. It was a rainy night. They had just finished making love.

"All women are alike." It slipped from him before he realized he was replaying an old quarrel with Janice. He was a little drunk . . . must have been a Saturday.

He felt her getting up. The one lamp in the room was on his side. He fumbled for the switch and found it in time to see Sara standing at the foot of the bed holding her underpants in one hand while she pulled on her jeans.

"How original." Her voice trembled, then turned hard.

"You realize I could say the same about all men . . . if I were simple-minded." Her long blond hair caught under her sweater.

Reaching behind her, she pulled it free in one short habitual motion.

He grabbed her just before she got to the front door.

"I don't want another woman."

"Why not? Anyone will do."

"No. Come on back in here." He pulled her in the bedroom. She slapped him then. He backed away for a second, caught her around the waist with both arms, and threw her on the bed. Rolling over, she jumped to her feet on the opposite side.

"Don't ever hit me in the face again, Sara."

"I won't. Don't worry."

She ran out into the rain and would have nothing to do with him. He had to win her back, and it took weeks, a month, at least, but he won her — every time. No other woman had ever provoked him as much as she did, and no one had so delighted him. They fought about everything — whether it was right for him to stay in Mexico or not, dumb things they said to each other, the dog, whether to go to a party or not. Sometimes they wrestled on the floor as he'd wrestled with his brothers when they were young. Once Sara threw a cup at him. They both laughed when it crashed against a wall. Then he tackled her and accidentally knocked her head against the table. After that they were more careful, but they still fought. It was against all the rules, the ones he'd been brought up by, the ones he'd made for himself, to hit a woman even though she'd hit him. Sara wasn't at all interested in his rules. She had brothers herself and needs of her own. Though he did not hit her, he wrestled with her, pinned her to the floor, to the bed. All of his resentment overflowed and was subdued in these fights, for they fell together.

The jeep bumped on up the mountain side. Popo changed as they got closer. Blue in the distance, it turned gray and deep rust — the colors of volcanic slag — closer. Dormant since sometime in the forties when ash erupted in the crater, people apparently had forgotten that it was ever active. In Cortes' day it was said that his soldiers made gunpowder by mining brimstone from the crater of the volcano. A great many things were said. Legends multiplied in Mexico. Ixta, the white lady — Sara gave him the translations — also called the maiden, would sleep until Popo, the smoking mountain, the warrior, woke. Their mountains had almost as many appellations as their gods. He'd concluded that the little of the country's early history he knew began in mythology as did most histories except American unless one counted American Indian mythology. He didn't. That belonged to another culture, not to the "land of the pilgrim's pride." Yet there was a whole reverse side to Mexico — the modernity that produced crazy furniture and magnificent new architecture — hotels that were constructed on the same lines as Mayan temples, massive university buildings that mimicked ball courts and pyramids, white cones rising out of factories that copied Popo rising from the earth. Monumentally, brutally, the new buildings flared up, and within the depths of Mexico City ran the subway which skirted a pre-Hispanic ruin. He'd taken the subway when he was there. Sara wouldn't. She got pinched too often.

He glanced in her direction then turned his attention to the road again. When he was twelve his father had taught him to drive their pickup on the farm's dirt roads. "You have to know how," he told him. "Out here something could happen. I want you to be able to drive in for help if it does." Nothing had happened, no farm accidents, no hunting accidents though they all went bird hunting every fall. Bad tempered as his father was, he was also extremely careful.

Tim learned to drive up and down the little hills, through ruts, sand, mud, snow, ice, rain, mist, to concentrate, to take his foot off the brake, gun the motor, and scoot through wet places. He must have known every rock on those roads by the time he was thirteen. And he remembered the incredulous visitor asking, "You let that child drive?" Later his father said, "City man," with the kind of contempt he usually reserved for stupidity.

He'd known he would leave the farm, known he and his two brothers would have to. It was his father's land which he ruled like a feudal lord, one who demanded absolute obedience from anyone who stepped under his roof. In truth the place wouldn't support all of them; though it might have taken care of one more, no one wanted to stay.

"What are you frowning about, Tim?"

"I was remembering my father, thinking how he runs a kind of banana republic in East Texas. Actually he raised corn and soybeans when I was growing up. Now he's turned to cattle mostly. Last time I was home he told me he seemed to be in the grass business."

He fell silent again. He'd told her about his family. How well did he actually know his parents? Sometimes people involved with each other were the most ignorant. At first he'd thought Janice left him simply because she hated Mexico. In her round childish hand she wrote to him from Fort Worth saying she was tired of being a professor's wife, tired of being the dummy. She confessed she had to look up dummy, probably because it was one of those words she didn't want to know how to spell. He smiled when he remembered her self-awareness. Maybe, she said, he married her only so one person in the world would always be looking up to him. Maybe he had. If so it was a bad reason to marry. Why did it take so long to discover the bad reasons? It was like listing the real causes of wars once they were over.

For lunch they stopped by a small waterfall which ran beneath ferns to splash on rocks hundreds of feet below. Lying on his back staring at the little clouds circling Popo, he felt more at ease with himself and this strange world than he had for weeks. It was often like that. Once he was outside, once he was away from the university, away from houses, he was all

143

right. When he was a boy he'd wanted to be a forest ranger, to work in the mountains. Instead he'd gone to the University of Texas then to Columbia. How was it, he wondered as he often did, that a man's life went a certain way?

He'd gotten the job in Mexico by bumping into it. Out of graduate school with no particular prospects, he'd persuaded Janice to leave the children with her mother and come with him. They hadn't had a vacation in six years. Mexico City was near and relatively cheap. They had a little money saved. In a burst of high spirits, they went. To talk Janice into going had required some time. Like a lot of people, she had only visited the border towns. Large or small, they remained dusty, chaotic places to do a day's shopping and escape.

Mexico City impressed her at first, then she decided she hated the traffic, couldn't stand the air pollution, and the noise was unbearable. A bus ride brought them to Cholula. A long, rambling walk took him to the small university just outside town. Yes, they did need a historian. No, it didn't matter that he couldn't speak Spanish. He would have students who already spoke English . . . of course they would use him for practice, and they had.

They had. He was more of an English teacher than a history teacher.

A rustling in the grass disturbed him. Quail? The Indians shot or trapped nearly every bit of game available. Ammunition was expensive, so the men used snares when they ran out. They were cheap and efficient. The few rabbits he'd seen all looked like they were running faster than the ones he'd grown up with in Texas. If anybody could live off the land, the Indians in these mountains could. He'd have to give them that. He would like to spend a couple of weeks hunting with them. Ah, but they overdid everything. Used it all up, trashed it all up. There were fields full of wastepaper. Plastic choked the creeks. Women washing clothes spread them to dry on the rocks by the water while their empty detergent bottles floated in the stream.

Sara told him he was too impatient.

"They have a lot of things to do here. You know that. It can't all be taken care of at once."

"I know. But why do they have to foul up the country while they're doing it?"

"You have to live with plastic a while before you know the damage it does. What makes you think people in the U.S. are cured of throwing it around? You've forgotten."

He looked over at Sara as she slept curled against him on the blanket. She was never as alert as he was, never heard odd noises in the night, nor did she watch the sky for weather signs — city girl, country boy, the old mismatch fallen side by side in a foreign country. He sighed, stretched, and looked around him. Nothing but bright colored birds. He didn't know their names. It was like being a little boy again. Today I saw a red bird and a yellow bird. Sara might be able to tell him their Spanish names . . . meaningless words. Rustlings again. What was it? There were no deer in this forest. And deer didn't make that kind of noise. He sat up. Three Indians stepped quietly out of the woods and surrounded them. Glancing toward the road he saw a fourth waited on the other side of the jeep. They were all wearing machetes in their belts, all had on the usual heavy straw sombreros, dirty white shirts, nondescript ragged pants, sandals. He looked at their eyes, for at least one pair he could see into. They were all hidden, or were focusing on something else, refusing to look at him. No one seemed to have a gun or pistol.

"Sara," he whispered. "Wake up. We're in trouble."

"What is it? What do you want?" She scrambled to her knees then to her feet. "What do they want?" Pushing her hair away from her cheek with one hand, she said, "Buenas tardes."

One man stepped forward a little and murmured something. A curse? There was no telling. He was slightly taller than the others. Was he the leader? As he spoke again, Tim caught Sara's hand and backed slowly toward the jeep which he'd parked just off the road on the same side they'd been picnicking. The tone of the leader's voice . . . must be a curse. How long, he tried to think. . . . How long had it been since he'd seen another vehicle? An hour at least. And that was a cart, one of those with two big wooden wheels, and it wasn't coming up the mountain. It was only an old man hauling cabbages to the market.

"Sara, what is that guy saying?"

"I . . . I don't understand. It's a language I don't know. Nahuatl maybe. It sounds a bit like that . . . lots of s's. He's so nervous that he could be speaking English and I wouldn't understand it. Why are you pulling me backward?"

"Sara, try, please to get him to speak Spanish and keep moving toward the jeep. We are in real danger. We have to get out of here."

"All right, but I don't think — "

"Please, you must. This time, you must."

"Can I get the blanket? What about the basket?"

"Leave them."

The men came slowly forward. No one reached for anything, but Tim could feel them waiting for the moment to draw out their machetes. He had a perfectly clear picture of his .45 resting in his top right-hand bureau drawer while he had nothing, nothing to use as a weapon but the jack handle and that was in the jeep. A lot of good a jack handle would be against a machete. He'd never felt as defenseless or angry in his life. He thought of reaching for rocks on the road. Ah, what good would that do!

Three of the men came closer as if their steps were synchronized, as if they were counting on a last minute rush.

He reached the door and pushed Sara inside.

"Crawl over the gear shift. Hurry."

"Ok! Ok!"

He jumped in after her digging with sweaty fingers for the keys in his jeans' watch pocket. The men crowded around the hood as if they were going to prevent him from leaving. Did they know how to open it? Did they know enough to pull wires?

"What do you suppose they want?" Sara said in a tranquil musing voice.

"You, I guess. You and the jeep." He couldn't stop to think. Jamming the key in, he heard the motor's comforting roar. He wheeled the jeep around. Two of the men ran before him. Twenty yards below one threw himself down across the road.

"Tim! Don't!"

"You want — ? You want to be raped? Murdered?"

"No! I don't want you to kill that man either!" She shouted.

He gunned the motor and drove downhill as fast as he could with Sara screaming something in Spanish out the open window on her side.

The man rolled out of the way just before the front tires . . . except for his hand. Did he run over his hand? Tim looked back to see him dusting himself off. The other three were approaching him. One shook his fist in the air, the old sign of vengeance. Vaguely nauseated and triumphant at the same time, he turned toward Sara. "What were you hollering at them?"

"That you were crazy."

"Those men were going to kill us."

"How do you know?"

"Things like that happen here."

"We could have tried to find out what they wanted. You felt threatened, Tim. I let you scare me. Maybe all they wanted was a lift to the nearest village."

"Hitchhikers don't crawl out of the woods and surround you without a word. Goddamn, Sara, you could at least be happy you haven't been raped."

"You could at least think of alternatives. What if one of them had a sick wife or child back there in the woods and he didn't know how to tell us? You think you're the only person in the world who has trouble with Spanish? Some of these people are so isolated they never learn it."

"All right." He slowed the jeep. "Since you can think of so many other possibilities, I'll turn around and we'll run through it again. I'll drive back. We'll get out of the jeep. You pick up the blanket, get the basket. And — "

"We can't," she sighed. "You almost killed a man back there. That changes everything."

They rolled on down the mountain. He let the jeep take the curves faster than usual. She was probably right, and he was . . . maybe he was wrong. But there were bandits, plain, old-fashioned robbers, rapers, and killers. They did exist. The Martins, his friends from Guadalajara, had been forced to stop by three men on the road to Morelia, and if another car hadn't come along, they would have been shot. They were sure of that. So was he. The men on Popo had no guns. That's what Sara would say. But they had circled him, and her, and the jeep.

"Maybe they just wanted to be paid off," Sara said. "I think if they had been offered — "

"A bribe?"

"Yes, they . . . maybe they were asking for a *mordida* and then they would go away and quit scaring gringos."

He wound his way through the villages avoiding the ruts as best he could. There was no way to avoid the carts. Pulled by bony old horses, empty or full, they moved at a slow amble. Still mulling over the incident on the mountain, hopelessly frustrated by ambiguity, he shifted and reshifted gears, sounded his horn, and shouted, "Move it! Move over!" Shouting made him feel a little better.

When they got back to the compound Sara asked to be dropped off at her casita. She was tired, she said.

"Driving up and down that mountain is exhausting. The roads twist so I hardly know which way to lean. I feel like someone has been punching me in the ribs all afternoon."

Watching her walk to her door, he knew by the way she carried herself — the rigidity of her shoulders, head tilted back just a little — that she would probably leave him again.

He might not see her until just before she left Mexico . . . if she bothered to let him know then. In six months she'd be gone. He would be lonely without her. The rainy season was just starting. No more sitting in front of the fire with Sara. He frowned as he got out of the jeep. Maybe he ought to just go and get her, carry her back to his place, carry her kicking and screaming. No. Wrestling was something they did when they were friends.

"Sara!" He called without knowing he was going to.

She turned around.

"I . . . ah — " He walked slowly to her. "I don't know what was going on up there. I . . . I did think they were threatening us. Remember the Martins?"

"Yes." Her voice sounded carefully neutral.

"I thought about them . . . about you. I really believed they might try to — "

"Yes, you said. Tim, I don't suppose we'll ever understand what those men wanted."

"I don't know what anyone's likely to do down here." He took her hand.

"I don't know what anybody's going to do anywhere." She smiled briefly.

"I better let you go. You're tired."

"I'll be ok tomorrow."

He let her hand go. "All right."

Driving back to the house, he saw an enormous full moon rising. It never looked real here. It was too yellow, too large, too dramatic like the mariachis bellowing their sentimental songs. Everything was too much — too much pepper in the food, too much rain when they had it, too much bloody history, too many bloody revolutions, too much poverty, too much plastic, too many mountains, too many languages, too much corruption, too much violence. It was excessive, Mexico was, all that he knew of it.

And what could he make of himself if he left? Alligator wrestler, truck driver, auctioneer, kennel keeper, house painter. What did it matter? Some other history professor could come down to Cholula. He had to go back to his own violent country where he knew the curses people were mumbling and the words to the songs they were singing.

The Gardener

A NEW GARDENER is working for the decorator across the street. The decorator's yard is a small one filled with ornamental shrubs, low growing ground cover, and large daisies which bloom one by one. Appearing so occasionally, they are unnatural intrusions like a crane stranded on one leg in the middle of town or a hen roosting on a parking meter. Because of the last winter's record breaking low temperatures, many of the plants are either dead or partially dead. The gardener neither notices nor seems to care that the pyracantha on the west wall displays a brown mass of leaves amidst a few green branches or that the monkey grass outlining the sidewalk to the decorator's front door is itself outlined in beige stems. Perhaps he does care about the wretched state of the shrubbery and borders but doesn't know what should be done. He appears to do little. He waters the ground most thoroughly and with it, a white styrofoam cup and clear plastic bag which have blown by to nestle in one corner over the ivy that may not be interested in surviving anyway. Is that the way the gardener looks at it? Difficult to say.

He's a young man, tall, has a Mexican look — dark-haired olive-skinned. But his origins might be otherwise; there are

tall, dark-skinned, dark-haired men in Saudi Arabia, Turkey,
Greece. I believe this one's more local though, Mexican after
all. He wears the troubled frown those men reserve for their
youth. The gardener doesn't seem to speak to anyone. He's so
antisocial he's an enigma, a constant question mark hovering
on the opposite corner. He stares over other people's shoulders. I speak when I'm going up the street, smile, nod, make
all the polite gestures allowed to people who've not been
introduced. He never returns the slightest greeting. But he
watches me from a distance. I feel his eyes on me as I park my
car, get out, and walk into the office. I'm a paralegal, assistant
to a lawyer, another woman. Most days I am also a secretary.
I fill out legal forms, type the lawyer's words and the wishes of
her clients on heavy white paper. I sometimes think most of
my life is spent making marks. Too disheartening a thought.
So I brush it away. I have nephews and nieces, friends and
relations. Two cats live with me. I have plenty to busy myself
with. It's only that the gardener so often crosses my field of
vision, or I cross his.

He takes his breaks in a peculiarly public place, a set of steps
leading to nothing, a blank west wall opposite my east windows. That's where those steps rise. Why does he choose this
spot? It's shady, yes. Perhaps he wants to be out of the decorator's sight. That's not hard. All the windows on the west
side are covered with wooden lattice work. Perhaps he wants
to be out of my sight, not difficult either for half the year. In
the spring and summer the sun shines so brightly that I can't
see anyone at all from my windows. He's present when I come
and sometimes when I go. He doesn't work till five as I do
most days. Some days I work till seven. It's hard to tell when
he works till.

He eats his lunch, takes all his breaks sitting on top of those
three steps leading to the blank wall; surely a door must have
been there once. Other people's renovations are frequently
puzzling. The gardener is alone all the time or was until yes-

terday when another young man, Mexican looking, shorter, with broader features, was by his side. For the first time I saw him laugh. He looked quite natural doing it. I believe he knew I was watching.

He plants nothing but waters assiduously, waters all the time because the bad weather continues. We are in the midst of a drought. In May we were six inches behind our allotted measure of rain; now in August, we lack twelve. Even in the best of times not enough is allotted. Water is an obsession in the Southwest. There must be twenty words for wet. We try to live like Moors though there aren't enough fountains in people's houses unless one counts the lawn sprinklers. The gardener's sprinklers are circles with spouts in the center. The corner sidewalk that holds the decorator's property in its unending L is, I am certain, a public thoroughfare. Even so the gardener's small sprinklers wet the sidewalk and may wet you. Unintentionally. He has to water the English ivy that borders the curb and creeps to the sidewalk.

One day he is out front when I go by. From habit, I nod. He nods back.

"Morning," I say, not wanting to say too much. Since he's never nodded he would, I fear, be easily frightened.

"It is afternoon." He corrects me gravely, quietly, rather like a patient elder child corrects a failing parent.

"Yes, of course." I stand there transfixed, a woman forty-eight, medium frame, medium everything — mouse-blond hair, green-brown eyes. Nondescript. Above average intelligence according to the standard tests. But what do they matter? What do years of social training matter? I can't think of a word to push us across this tentative bridge we've begun to build, the bridge across the water which is wetting my ankles. He's difficult, terribly difficult. I've suspected that. I didn't suspect myself. Why was I so unaware that the force of another personality would hit me like this? How could I know

that this tall young man's handsome face would assail me so?
I break away from his eyes and say, "I . . . my office is across
the street."

"I know."

Without a word, he turns his back on me and walks away.
I am reminded of adolescent rudeness in his catlike turn and
stalk.

I stoop to lift the plastic bag and the styrofoam cup from
their resting place in the ivy.

"You forgot something."

"What?"

"You forgot this stuff. Its been here over a month now." I
let both objects drop on the sidewalk. Why? I am a woman
who seldom knowingly provokes anyone. I am, as I have said,
nondescript. I look like I'm the sole support of somebody. I
look like a woman who sings in the church choir every Sunday. I look like every teacher you ever had whose face you
can't remember.

My looks are not important. The gardener's are. He is so
tall, so aloof, so handsome, so angry. Anger pushes lines in his
face, and I see he looks younger than he actually is.

"Put it back."

"No." I kick the styrofoam cup so it bounces in small arcs
over the sidewalk.

"Don't." He whispers.

"It's just an old cup." I kick it merrily again.

"He'll see." He points toward the door.

"The decorator? He won't care. He's only interested in the
insides of houses. Tell him I'm mad . . . just a mad woman."

The gardener walks beside me. I'm pleased, terribly pleased.

"He won't believe me. You work over there?" He nods at
the small house that has been made into our office, a convenient metamorphosis for this area so near the capitol.

"Yes. I work for a lawyer."

"Maybe you are one too?"

"No, I'm not one too. I'm mad." I find I enjoy relieving

myself of the responsibility of being rational. "And I think you are also. You're not a gardener. Your pyracantha is a disaster and your pittisporum is a mess. It should have been pruned by the end of March by the man who used to work here. Now it's the end of August. The growing season is over, and those bushes are rotting. I'm not going to speak about the monkey grass except to say there's monkey business if ever I saw it."

"Monkeys?" As I suspected, he doesn't know the name of anything. He might be, as we say here, wet, meaning wet-back, meaning illegal alien, meaning nothing very much. They're all over the place. Actually the entire state of Texas was once theirs. It's a long border; crossing it is a natural proclivity.

"This is monkey grass." I point a disdainful finger at it. "This," I gesture toward the bush withering against the wall, "is pyracantha."

"That's a daisy." He says and smiles at the top-heavy flower drooping before us.

"Yes, and there's something wrong with it."

"I will water it today."

I shake my head. "Too much chlorine in the city water. Rainwater has more nitrogen and everything here needs it."

"I can't make the rain."

"I didn't think so."

"It is true I do not know the names of the plants. Are you going to tell?"

"Who would I tell?"

"Him." He nods toward the decorator's door, looks back at me and adds, "Anyone."

"No."

"A thousand thanks."

His courtesy is pleasantly old-fashioned. We are at the edge of the sidewalk. I put one foot on the street and push myself away from the curb, away from this handsome troubled young man. Yes, I can tell he's troubled. I am always magnetized to the difficult ones — the alcoholics, the marvelously neurotic,

the men with secrets they need to reveal. But not to me. I
have learned that ignorance is preferable to certain sorrows. I
turn my back on him. What is it to me if the decorator has a
decorative gardener? It's a way of life, isn't it? A role that can
easily be played. Enter stage right. Scowl. Water. Exit stage
left. Smile. Maintain good posture. Don't stoop, don't get
your hands dirty. The names of the plants do not matter.
Maintain good relations with the neighbors.

The next afternoon I find a red and white carnation in a
styrofoam cup full of water on the ground near my car. Like an
old drunk, it leans against the door ready to wilt and die in the
August heat. We are proud of the height of temperatures here,
we commit degrees and dates to memory and bring out those
red hot pokers to prod newcomers. The carnation does not
flourish in this state. They have to be flown in from some
cooler area. I know the gardener has placed it here for me. His
broad-faced friend must work in a florist shop or at one of the
new groceries where cut flowers are sold. He's the produce
man who's also in charge of flowers. Yes. And he gave this
one to the gardener to give to me. I grab up the carnation,
clench my teeth over its stem. Carmen getting in her car.
Carmen leaving her office. She must have worn her flowers in
her hair. It's impossible to drive with a long moist stem drib-
bling over you. I roll down the window and fling the flower at
the decorator's sidewalk. I will not be wooed with gifts from a
bogus gardener.

The next morning he is sitting on the steps to our back
door, the place I usually enter our office.

"What are you doing here?"

"You did not like the flower."

"Give your flower to some other woman."

"I want you," he says and does not smile.

Like the carnation, I wilt. I need to be loved as much as
anyone. Two cats are cold company even at 104 degrees on
August 25. People who live by themselves can afford to be

erratic. I will take on this young gardener, troubled as he may be. Already I know what he wants. Papers. He desires an immigration permit, a green card, a real social security number. I will help him. Yes, I know also what will happen next. He'll throw me over in favor of a young and beautiful though slightly plump third generation Chicana. Her grandparents will have come here from some stony soil in the sierras near San Luis Potosi or the scrubby desert of Chihuahua, and she will hardly speak Spanish. This Delores, this Tina, this María.

It does not matter. What matters is that the gardener offers me a bouquet of all the decorator's drooping daisies — evidently he has been saving them — and I accept.

The Greats

N MY mother's family Great Uncle Ambrose is known as "the one who painted the fence blue." He did it when he was drunk, and everyone else had gone to town one remote Saturday in the early 1930s. The fence was a typical Middle Tennessee white post-and-rail arrangement surrounding five acres of the farm's front lawn, a small pasture for children, Shetland ponies, dogs, trees, and swings. No one knew why Uncle Ambrose was drunk. He was a visitor from Charleston. Perhaps he brought some sorrow with him, or some sudden joy demanded celebration. But why did he choose to paint the fence?

My grandfather, I was told, said, "By God, Ambrose, I wish you'd taken on the barn. It needed painting." (He didn't have much leeway for comment since he got drunk and did strange things himself.)

No one could tell me if Great Uncle Ambrose finished the job. When I was six, ten years or so after the deed was done, I used to get stuck on a mean-tempered Shetland who preferred grazing a corner of the lawn to trotting children about. When I wasn't bawling for someone to come and lead the pony away — quite logically I feared he'd bite me as he'd bitten one of my cousins already — I was looking for splinters of blue underneath the white rails. Other coats of paint and weather had washed it all off. Though I inquired, no one could explain Great Uncle Ambrose's choice of color, nor could they remember why there were buckets of blue paint at the farm.

Grandfather Moore was a neat farmer. His place looked like the pictures in my first grade reader, or rather some of the outbuildings did. There was a log smokehouse, a red barn for livestock, a gray weathered wood house where "the help" lived, and a gray tobacco barn. The house was rose-red brick, two-story, ante-bellum — too southern for *Dick and Jane*. All were kept in good order though Grandfather collected things. Any number of half-filled buckets of paint were stored in the livestock barn along with a dilapidated buggy, old mule col-lars, singletrees, other bits of harness, and machinery. Am-brose might have wandered in there in the midst of a drunken reverie and picked up the first bucket of paint available.

However the fence painting happened, Moore family my-thology, which concentrates on deeds and neglects motiva-tions, prevents further inquiry. And Great Uncle Ambrose, himself, returned to Charleston where he died before I was old enough to ask the right questions.

Great Aunt Eula is "the one who went to California to buy movie houses." This was sometime before 1927 when *The Jazz Singer* signaled the beginning of "talkies." Whatever possessed her? She was a middle-aged woman, married to an indulgent man. My grandmother said, "Maybe she was tired of playing lady up there in Kentucky." (Her guess was reliable as any since she played lady emphatically herself.) Great Aunt Eula was also the only one of the Moores who knew anything about family history. Except for their own memories, none of them were in the least interested in genealogy. "Eula knows all that," they would say. After a short visit to Tennessee the family chronicler arrived in Los Angeles where she did indeed buy a movie house, for she wrote to my grandparents offering them free passes to all the shows if they would only come out.

My grandfather scorned the idea as "one of Eula's notions" though Grandmother Moore wanted to go, a desire that categorized her as a great a daydreamer as Eula. California was a good place for her, but no one else was supposed to fall under her spell. Grandmother Moore did allow my mother to answer Eula's summons. "Come on out and I'll get you in the movies," she said. Mother went to L.A., was photographed intensively by a friend of Eula's, and came home after a month without even seeing a movie. Years later she said, "There was never time. We always had to rush off to meet someone or other who made a lot of promises." The statement was made without rancor. Apparently she'd had a good time and she'd never believed Aunt Eula's expectations could turn her into an actress.

"You know Eula. She had to have her way." So say present-day survivors. She was, according to them, headstrong and inclined to overreach herself in business matters. When she was quite old one of her nephews had to rescue her. He found her sitting on a sofa surrounded by the rest of her furniture in the yard of a house she was renting. She refused to use the word "evicted" to describe her problem. "Temporarily low on funds," she explained. She died in California, and as far as I can find out, no one in the family ever entered one of her movie houses if, indeed, she ever bought more than one.

I don't think they were particularly angry at her. Great Aunt Eula simply left their sphere. My grandfather owned land, real estate in town, mules, horses, hogs. A woman who wanted to buy movie houses was, in all senses of the term, "outlandish" even though she was his sister.

She was gone before I ever got to California, but I like to think of her sitting in a darkened movie house in Los Angeles watching Mary Pickford, Charlie Chaplin, Theda Bara, Rudolph Valentino, and all the rest. And I also like to believe she enjoyed seeing *The Mark of Zorro* and *The Three Muske-*

teers a whole lot more than she liked icing tea cakes and collecting dates for the Moore family tree especially since they disdained her efforts.

Great Aunt Eula and Great Uncle Ambrose vanished. Great Uncle Howard, who ventured out of the mountains of East Tennessee is, peculiarly, still with us. He was visiting my grandfather and died "of a fever" while staying at the farm. As children my cousins and I used to try to guess which of the house's four bedrooms he died in and what fever he died of. Was it typhoid, poliomyelitis, meningitis? No one could tell us. "People died of fevers back then," said my grandmother, exasperated by such scientific research. (Self-interest was involved. We were all terrified of polio and wanted to keep away from dormant germs.) Neither could anyone tell us exactly where Great Uncle Howard was buried. "Somewhere in the family plot," they all said. The family plot has a general tombstone proclaiming MOORE; however, again for reasons no one can explain, he has no private stone, so when anyone dies Uncle Howard is "the one who has to be found." Some cemetery worker must probe the ground with a rod until Uncle Howard's casket is located. Why wouldn't my grandfather buy his brother a tombstone? Did he dislike him? Was he hiding him from the law? Or was the tombstone merely one of those details grandfather didn't get around to taking care of before his own early death?

I thought once to ask for contributions for Uncle Howard's stone, but I realized that the family preferred to let him stay as he is. Finding Great Uncle Howard is a welcome distraction when somebody else dies. And it is a ritual.

Though careless of ancestry, the Moores accept him as they do the other greats, their eccentric, willful, and finally, mysterious kin.

The Grands

HE GROUND MIST eddied around the mule's legs. He walked slowly toward a farm-house as if aware that the man on his back was asleep. Behind the hills the moon set, casting long shadows on rows of cotton already stripped. Leftover bits dotted the dark earth, fluttered from the bolls' dry hulls, caught the eye of the mule's rider as he woke. Rising slightly, he touched the fiddle tied to the back of his saddle. As he reached the front porch steps, he shook his head then shouted.

"Hal–loo! Hal–loo!"

The front door opened quickly, but he could not make out the figure holding the lamp.

"Can you tell me where Edgar Moore lives?"

"Edgar Moore?" a woman's voice answered.

"Yes."

"Mr. Moore, this is your own house, you fool. Get off that mule and come inside."

He slid off the mule, untied his fiddle, pulled the girth free, and with the same hand wrestled the saddle and blanket to the porch. Tucking the fiddle under one arm, he moved to the mule's head, already lowered, slid the bridle off, tossed it, reins dragging, on top of the saddle. For a moment he considered the steps. Five, or were there six? He took every other one in defiant leaps. As he fell over the doorsill, he held the fiddle up in his right hand, then gently both arm and fiddle sank to the carpet.

Kate Moore looked down at him. She had on a new night dress which she saw he would not notice. Her long, dark hair was covered with a paisley scarf to keep it unmussed till church time tomorrow. She turned away and put the lamp down on a table by the door. Gathering the white dress around her legs, she sat down on the third step of the stairs. For ten minutes she waited. The figure at her feet did not stir. She stood up, carefully curved his legs out of the way, and pushed the door to. Moving deliberately, she stepped over to pick up the lamp, then carrying it before her, she walked to their bedroom. A mule loose on the front lawn, her husband so drunk he couldn't move out of the entry hall. Such depravity stopped at her threshold. She locked the door.

It was 1906. My grandmother Moore told me this incident — part of it — long after Grandpa was dead, long after I'd left Tennessee, had married and gone to New Mexico. Part of it she may have imagined. Mine is a family of tale tellers, anecdote swappers, believers in the word, for we have used the word to know each other's lives. But the word often fails. There are lapses, year-long pauses, lies perhaps. And who's to set matters straight? Whoever is left. There are not many of us.

Leaning back in her chair fifty-four years later, my grandmother drifted away for a moment as old people do when telling a story they know well, yet at these times she seemed to be musing over some fragment she did not choose to reveal.

"And the fiddle wasn't broken?" I asked.

"No, would have served him right if it had been. Would have served him right if I'd never opened the front door. He'd been at a country dance right after harvest. Big, noisy gatherings. I seldom went. Mr. Moore always wanted to go so he rode off to play the fiddle for them. In those days they paid the fiddler with liquor, moonshine most likely. That's why Mr. Moore came home, rather the mule brought him home, in that disgraceful condition."

"Miss Kate," Grandpa called her, twenty-two in 1906, seventy-six when she decided to tell me the tale, remained a formidably respectable woman. A churchgoer, organizer of Sunday schools, a house cleaner, and a collector of cut-glass and porcelains which stood on what-not shelves, a piece of furniture all children were forbidden to approach, she was described by everyone in the family with one word — particular. Though reputedly the best cake baker in the county, she detested cooking. Her ideas about what ladies did and did not do led her away from the farm to her house in town as often as possible. She knew how to make lye soap and wring a chicken's neck but she preferred, as she grew older, to forget such skills. She continued, however, to call Grandpa, dead thirty years before her, "Mr. Moore" all her long life.

Did the formality mark the distance between them? He was ten years older. Or was it merely the custom at that time for women to refer to their husbands as "Mr." in public while reserving first names for private conversations? Both of these I suspect. And there was yet another reason — inverse snobbery. By continual use of this title and by other means — she insisted he should wear a suit rather than overalls to town — Grandmother tried to reconstruct Grandpa. He would, she was determined, become a gentleman, an act of will bound to fail. Grandpa's friends called him "Sog," a name given to him as a child after he fell into a half-empty barrel of sorghum molasses. When told that his station in life demanded a suit he said, "Miss Kate, I will cover myself with a suit for weddings, funerals, going to the bank for a loan, and other great occasions but I will not ruin my business by wearing one. Mule traders wear overalls like mule buyers do."

It was a spurious argument since he had many other occupations; however, it served his purpose. She gave up on the suit but not the "Mr." Though she never said so, it was apparent Grandmother felt she had married beneath her. She was an Allen from Virginia, a designation involving, as far as we could tell, contriving to act as if one's breeding and social position were more important than money, especially when the family fortune had fallen to the poverty level.

Some of "the other Moores," alas, included a distant uncle in an equally distant penitentiary and a brother who made moonshine in one of the local hollows. Grandmother never uttered their names, nor did anyone else in her presence. In fact I did not know of their existence till I was thirty-two, and Uncle Phillip, an in-law, told me Miss Kate had pruned the family tree, lopsidedly as it turned out. She continued to visit her own brother who, besides working as a circus roustabout and running the Silver Slipper Saloon somewhere in Oklahoma, later opened a liquor store in the Texas Panhandle. He was excused because it was a legitimate business located at a safe distance from Allen territory. Texas, to her mind, was the wild west, a suitable place for a wild brother.

Grandpa also still went to see his brother, privately we supposed. Except for lineages of mules, horses, and birddogs, Mr. Moore did not care about breeding. Somewhere during their marriage, early I'd venture, Grandpa gave up discussing asses, mares, stallions, and bitches when Grandmother dropped the Allens of Virginia. By the time I was old enough to notice such omissions, she seemed to have lost interest in ancestry altogether.

Grandpa Moore died in 1938 when he was sixty-three and I was three, too young to ask him the truth of those surmises or any others that were passed on to me. Only a few of the immediate family are left. Age, accident, and illness carried off Grandmother, my mother, the only son George. Aunt Lucy, her husband Phillip, and their son Fergus remain in Tennessee. I married and moved first to Texas, then to New Mexico, but I fly back to visit my relatives, compelled, I imagine, by the almost atavistic instinct of kinship that knots some families together. Air hours are short; movement through time is long. The moment I leave New Mexico I know I'm flying into a sepia-toned world peopled with beloved though elusive ghosts. Certain characteristics remain distinct while others are exaggerated, softened, forgotten, or changed entirely depending on who's telling the story. What is it we are after? No one seems to desire the whole truth, whatever that may be.

We have never ceased speculating about Grandpa's death, which was admittedly strange. He was run over by the Interurban, an electric trolley which ran from Nashville to Franklin, a nearby county seat. Part of the tracks bordered his farm, so he often rode home from the fields. What was he doing on those well-known tracks? Could he possibly have gotten stuck? He was diabetic. Did he fall into a coma right there? Did he get drunk and fall asleep on the tracks? Uncle Phillip brought this up, but nobody else agreed with his theory. Was Grandpa suicidal? Why would he have been? None of these questions have ever been answered to anyone's satisfaction. In 1938 autopsies were seldom performed to settle family curiosity. The suggestion of one would have, no doubt, shocked my grandmother. The Interurban had run over Grandpa. That was enough.

He is so much alive in everyone else's imagination that I cannot imagine his death. During childhood summers at the farm I'd seen the trolley swerving along making clicking noises on the tracks. Since then I've seen those abandoned tracks. I've seen the place Grandpa Moore lay across them. Where was the mustachioed villain? The peril was evident. Oh, it was absurd!

Like drowning in two feet of water, or choking to death on a fish bone, or dying from a concussion after slipping in a bathtub. Nevertheless, the Interurban ran over Grandpa Moore.

His farmhouse was two-story, faded red brick. The sloping roof of the long front porch divided the front of the house in half. Inside, underneath the stairs, was a closet with a fake floor and space enough between it and the cellar ceiling for a man to hide, a secret place never revealed to children of the family for fear something might happen to one of us if we used it. When Grandmother finally told me, I was twenty-eight and had children of my own to protect, yet I felt cheated.

"What a grand place for hide-and-seek it would have been."

"You might have gotten stuck. The hinges were rusty. Anyway you most certainly would have been afraid in that small dark space. You would have been hysterical. Screaming and crying."

"I wouldn't have."

"Some other child would've."

"I wonder who built it?"

"We never knew. Perhaps it was added. The farmhouse was old. I forget when it was built exactly, sometime before the Civil War though."

"Perhaps Confederate soldiers were hidden there."

"Aren't you the romantic!"

"Or it was part of the underground railway."

"More than likely it was meant to hide valuables. Silver, and jewelry, and such."

Wasn't it just as likely that Grandpa hid his whiskey there, and she knew it though she wasn't supposed to? I stared at her. She had dark eyes, a small staunch figure. No matter what the season she wore a full corset. Her composure, her certainty about all matters of opinion, was broken only by laughter. I cannot remember seeing her cry until she was in her eighties and had had a cerebral hemorrhage. Yet I was not there to witness every moment of her life.

There were many secrets in the family, things not told for

years. Grandmother never told anyone where she met Mr. Moore, not even her own children. My cousin Fergus said he bet they met on a train. Fergus is "a little wild" his mother says, but he's my only first cousin. He drove our grandmother out to Santa Fe to my oldest child's christening, so naturally I like him. And I like his idea. Everybody rode trains then.

"How do you do, Miss — ? My name is Edgar Moore. I farm down around Franklin, Tennessee." Mr. Moore sat in the seat across from her.

"I don't know a thing about agriculture. I could hardly tell you if that was corn or cotton growing out there." She folded her white-gloved hands on her lap and looked out the window.

"Ladies needn't know about farming. Where are you from?"

"Virginia. Most of my family lives in Richmond. I have an aunt in Tennessee."

"Where?"

"Franklin." She twisted her fingers together. She had never ridden on a train alone before, much less spoken to a man while riding on one, but it seemed uncivil not to speak when he was sitting just across from her. Of course she would not give him her name. Fortunately Mr. Moore recognized the aunt when he and Miss Kate arrived at the station. In time, allowing a few days for her to recover from her journey, he came calling.

If they were both on the train from Richmond to Nashville in 1904, it was as innocent as that, I believe. How easy it is to believe one's own fictions. Perhaps they were not riding the train. Perhaps they met on some other occasion. He was an eligible bachelor, and she was a young woman in need of a husband. I'm certain they did not meet in church. Grandpa was a backslidden Methodist, one of those who attended Easter services if he went at all, while Grandmother was a Campbellite, a member of the Church of Christ, one of the fiercer

fundamentalist groups. Drinking, smoking, dancing, gam-
bling, and card playing were forbidden. So were musical in-
struments in church. To tune the congregation for hymn singing, the minister blew on a pitch pipe. The only amusement
during the service was reading the hymnal or lugubrious
funeral parlor advertisements on one side of the cardboard
fans.

Invariably the picture was of a long-haired, extremely gen-
tile Christ dressed in a white robe vaguely reminiscent of
garments worn by the choir in other churches. He was standing in a highly idealized garden of Gethsemane alone except
for a number of rose bushes in the foreground and cypress trees
in the background. I used to wonder about those heavy, red,
symmetrical roses. They were like no others I'd seen. Finally
I decided they were supposed to be heavenly flowers. The
message beneath ran: Your Friend In Your Hour Of Need.
Then there was the name and phone number of the funeral
parlor. As a child with a wide experience in visiting family
churches — all kinds of Protestants plus Catholics were rep-
resented — I found Grandmother's the most dour. However,
it suited her astringent needs which were most apparent in her
sense of decorum. To her the simplest act such as meeting a
man could be dangerous. One had to have a proper introduc-
tion by some family member or, lacking that, by a trusted
friend. Over-trained in social conventions, she had no training at all in being a farmer's wife. How did she adapt? I wish
I'd asked her during her lifetime, still the question isn't difficult. So much is already known it's easy for me to intuit her
answers.

"At the farm the front porch was a good deal of trouble
because children wanted to play out there. I would be in the
kitchen and Mr. Moore would come in carrying George. He
was about two then."

Both Grandpa's and George's faces were red, Grandpa's
from the sun, George's from bawling.

"Miss Kate, he's fallen off the porch again. Why can't you watch this child?" he shouted.

She shouted back, "I can't watch George and cook dinner at the same time. There are too many dangerous places around here. Watch him yourself."

"I'm hiring you a cook."

"High time!" Miss Kate turned her own reddened face back to the wood stove, a large black cast iron monster she despised every day all day every summer.

She was expecting my mother then. 1908. Pregnant, hot, often exhausted, she was in no humor to accommodate. George did not fall off the porch again. She sat on the porch swing, fanned herself, and watched him while Minnie took over the kitchen.

My grandmother and I never looked in the least alike. Our opinions seldom matched. Though I cry easily, perhaps our temperaments are somewhat the same. Children are easily influenced. I lived in the town house with her, Uncle George, and my mother during part of World War II. I wish I had a cook.

In his photograph Grandpa, curly-headed and long-nosed, looks like a sober, industrious squire. In many ways he was. A gold watch-chain stretched across a large belly. He had three hundred acres of rich Middle Tennessee land where he raised cotton, corn, alfalfa, tobacco, and the usual barnyard produce, hogs and chickens. He also had mules to trade and property in town to tend. Until Miss Kate made him take it down, he had a sign on his front gate reading *Trade in Your Old Mules for New*. After he died my grandmother lived for thirty years on his investments and had some money left over to leave to their children. In part he was another sort of person which accounted for a barely suppressed smile and definite laughter in his eyes in that photograph. As a child I simply thought he looked jolly. Fergus, five years older, knew better.

"Grandpa was a rascal. He taught me to chew tobacco when I was seven."

"Didn't you hate the taste of it?"

"Yes, but he convinced me it was something a man needed to know how to do. He taught me how to spit too. Put me up on a wagon seat with him, took me off to town to trade mules. On the way there and back he gave me cussing lessons. We had a wonderful time."

"What did Aunt Lucy say about that?"

"Mamma didn't know until too late. There was a whole side to Grandpa he didn't show to women."

Fergus has Grandpa's long nose and curly hair. He was working on the belly, said it came naturally since he had to stay up all night eating and drinking with his clients, country musicians who swept into Nashville to play at the Grand Ole Opry or hoped to play there. Like so many bats out of a cave blinded by light, they weren't really comfortable until dark, so Fergus kept his recording studio open till two or three in the morning. We were talking in his office, the single messiest place I've ever entered — this includes the slums of Naples and my children's bedrooms. Over two desks a hanging basket of red plastic geraniums dangled from a set of longhorn steer horns partially hiding a five-foot print of a tiger serenely marching through his jungle. A round table pushed to one side held stacks of poker chips, cards, a cluster of dirty glasses and ashtrays. File boxes sat on all but one seat of a couch. Next to them was a charro hat somebody had brought Fergus from Mexico. Plastic ferns caught dust in front of a window that was never opened.

Behind me in the next room was a well-stocked bar equally in shambles. People, most of them wearing blue jeans, wandered through the office to the bar to replenish drinks. Fergus nodded or waved as they came and went. Grandpa's gold watch, suspended under a glass globe, shone amid the chaos of papers, calculators, hunting knives, and one villainous looking carved coconut rolling around between the phones on his desk. The coconut had on an eye patch, a bit of blue bandana, and an earring, all attempts to transform it into a pirate's head. I counted three broken guitars in two corners; a busted drum took up one chair. In order to sit down, I had to prop my feet on a large carton of toilet paper, not that I minded. Fergus has always been like this, a collector and a keeper. The office was his version of Grandpa's barn, a jumble of harness, buggies, and everything that ever was a piece of farm equipment. Strictly his territory. No one disturbs Fergus' clutter but him. He lives in it like a bandit chief surrounded by his spoils.

"You know, Marianne, the only woman who ever caught sight of Grandpa's carrying on was Miss Kate, and she didn't know the half of it."

"How did they stay together all those years? Of course there were three children. But he was ten years older than she was — "

"People did then," said Fergus. He'd been divorced once and seemed perpetually on the edge of marrying again though he could never quite make up his mind to it. Compared to Fergus, I've led a sedate life, married for twenty-five years to the same man, mother of three. My husband and I run a horse ranch, a place near Santa Fe where we breed and raise quarter horses. Like Grandmother we have a house in town also.

"Of course," Fergus reminded me, "Miss Kate was his perfect opposite. He honored her quirks — built her that house in Franklin, paid for all kinds of help — and she put up with his . . . his good times."

And the bad times? Do we forget them too easily? "Sufficient unto the day is the evil thereof." Well, yes. We don't like to think of our grandparents as pitiable. They were though. For all her bossiness, my grandmother loved men, yet for thirty years she was a widow. During her last years she was quite mad. In her senility she confused me with my mother, another of her sorrows, a daughter dead in a plane wreck —

the reason why Fergus drove her to New Mexico. She
wouldn't fly. She had allergies, arthritis, her share of aches,
fevers, and anxiety attacks which she called "nerves."

As for Grandpa? I do know a mean old sow bit him in the
calf of his leg, and he had to use a cane for six months. He was
aware that his only son George hated farming. He was not
fond of either one of his sons-in-law. Hail flattened entire
alfalfa crops. Drought destroyed the cotton. Every kind of pest
invaded his fields. To the forces of nature, he remained a
stoic. ("The earth survives all weather," he said.) To the
forces within he was, I think, largely a stranger. He often
drank too much when he wasn't supposed to drink at all.
Diabetes made him melancholy. Some days he sat alone on
the steps to the hay loft and cursed. I never saw him there,
still I'm sure he must have done it, slumped there in the dark
barn, fanned his face with his hat, and cursed repetitively,
dully.

"Why didn't I ever hear Grandpa play the fiddle?" Aunt
Lucy is the only one I can ask.

"Oh, you were too young. No, let me think. He quit playing for the family sometime in the thirties. He'd go to his
room to play or sit out under a tree in the yard. I don't know
what made him do it, some argument he and Mother had, I
guess . . . something to do with fiddling and drinking. They
seemed to go together. But he used to play for us all on
Saturday nights — when we'd stay home to listen. He was the
only one in the family who knew how to play a musical in-
strument. Mother had a player piano. Remember?"

I did. It stood in a corner of the living room out at the farm
and was as forbidden to children as the what-not shelves. Field
mice had invaded it, eaten all the felt off the hammers,
chewed through rolls of paper. My grandmother's mute cultural pretension; it might as well have been a broken hay
mower.

"Your mother and father — before they married — Uncle

Phillip, and I used to dance on the front porch in the summers. No rugs were ever rolled up for dancing in Mother's
houses. George joined in when he was courting a girl. He was
always the caller. It wasn't the kind of music we wanted in the
twenties. Papa only knew square dance tunes, things like
Cotton-Eyed-Joe, The Virginia Reel, Shoofly. We wanted
saxophones, drums, trumpets . . . jazz."

It was easy to see them. Grandpa in a vest and shirtsleeves,
tapping his foot just outside the front screen door, light from
the entryway falling on his fiddle under his chin, moths flut-
tering toward the light. Three young men, three young
women dancing.

"Promenade all," George called, and they pranced all the
way to the swing, heels clattering on the wooden porch floor.
An owl hooted. The moon rose. At a distance the lawn's
familiar elms, maples, magnolias were outlined in black, and
the tops of the men's cars shone in the driveway. Grandpa
played while his children square danced before him wearing
flapper clothes. That was the only kind of dancing Miss Kate
allowed. The Charleston, the shimmy, the black bottom,
even the foxtrot were as religiously banned as the hip flask.

"Your father generally had some whiskey with him. Or if he
didn't, your Uncle Phillip did. I suspect George did too only
he couldn't very well offer his papa a drink. When we were
finished the men would go out to the cars and — "

"Where was Grandmother?"

"In the kitchen unpacking ice-cream. She had Minnie to
make it and George to crank it. She made the cake . . .
chocolate with a fudge icing or lemon with bits of shredded
peel in a white seven minute icing." She smiled. "Makes me
hungry to think about them. Your father and Phillip and Papa
sat on the porch steps chewing mints till she called them in."

Aunt Lucy is white-headed and slight. Fluttery as a small,
nervous bird. Uncle Phillip is short, pink-cheeked, white-
headed also. He likes the nostalgic tales but he insists, sensibly
as usual, "You're forgetting the bad years."

"Yes," Aunt Lucy sighed. "There were those Papa would plant, we'd have a drought, and there would be nothing to reap. Mother hated those times. She'd have to rent the town house and she couldn't go to Saratoga. Oh Lord, how she loved going to Saratoga Springs! So we'd just be stuck there on the farm gathering eggs and waiting for the weather to change. That's when Papa took off. I never knew where he went exactly. He'd be gone over a week sometimes." She drifted back to the kitchen to bring us some coffee.

"Hunting," Fergus winked at me and his father. "He went off hunting I expect."

We were sitting in another room full of Grandmother's dark Victorian furniture Aunt Lucy had inherited. Carved leaves, nuts, fruit protruded from the backs and arms; unyielding upholstery held us upright. The cut-glass shone on the sideboard and the what-not shelves were full of fussy porcelain figurines; a milkmaid, a shepherd, a harlequin, and men and women covered with lace who appeared to be engaged in a court dance sometime in the 1700s somewhere in Europe. There wasn't a single chicken, dog, pig, horse, or mule, no figure from my grandparents' daily lives. Naturally Grandmother wouldn't have wanted a figurine of the hired man or the cook, and the idea of a porcelain pig or mule in her parlor would have offended her. Propriety and beauty were Made In Dresden. Meanwhile Grandpa slopped hogs, traded mules, tilled the soil, bought property in town, and every once in a while, broke loose.

"I don't see any reason to disturb Mother's . . . um, view of the world. She's happy with it. But I'll tell you, Grandpa didn't do much hunting. He had a shack out in the woods where he went to do his serious drinking. One time he took the sheriff with him." Fergus laughed.

"Why?"

"Marianne," said Uncle Phillip, "You remind me of your mother, always wanting to know why this and why that. Until you came along she asked more questions than anybody in the family. No one knows why exactly. He thought the sheriff was working too hard maybe. Mr. Moore and some fellow were having an altercation on the square. The sheriff's office was right there. He stepped out to ask them to quiet down. Mr. Moore talked him into getting in the buggy with him. You wouldn't remember his horses. He had a fine pair of matched bays. Before the sheriff knew it, your grandpa had taken him out of the county. They spent three or four days in the woods eating country ham, biscuits, and redeye gravy, and drinking whiskey. Country ham creates a powerful thirst. Probably they did a little dove hunting too. Finally the sheriff mentioned he had to get back to town."

I sat in that upright chair thinking for a few minutes about a three- or four-day diet of country ham, redeye gravy, biscuits, and whiskey. There is absolutely nothing anybody can do to vary the taste of Tennessee country ham. Smoke cured, with hickory usually, heavily salted, it's first boiled for hours, baked, cooled, then cut into the thinnest possible slices which are eaten cold or fried in ham fat. After the first day maybe the whiskey helped. Or maybe Grandpa and the sheriff stumbled to the nearest farm and bought some eggs. Oh, it's not hard at all to search the country for groceries, not for me. I know that country, know what a hungry farmer and a sheriff might eat.

"Sog, I can't eat eggs."

"Can't?"

"Never could look a fried egg in the eye."

"Scrambled?"

"Them neither. My mama used to cook them with brains. With or without they still look suspicious to me."

The woman at the back door waited holding a bowl in her hands. Her hair was gray, her figure slack. She had on a loose brown shift. Miss Kate wouldn't have given her the time of day if she'd seen her in the country or in town.

"What about turnip greens, Ma'am? You got any turnip greens you'll sell us."

"Out there in the garden if you'll pick 'um. You won't be wanting the eggs then?"

"Let's cut that to a dozen 'stead of two."

"How you going to carry 'um?"

It was a poor place, a tenant farmer's shack with not a scrap of anything to waste, not a box, not a bit of paper.

He wrapped the eggs in some turnip green leaves and put them in his hat. The sheriff stuck the rest of the greens under the buggy's seat.

"Ain't we dandies, by God!" Sog roared as they took off.

"You're going to think so when one of them eggs breaks in your hat," said the sheriff.

"I wonder what Grandmother said when he got back?"

"I don't think she said anything much. They understood each other. He'd toe her mark just so long then he'd rip off," Uncle Phillip said. He must have wished sometimes that he'd ripped more himself. Most of his life he sold insurance and when he retired he kept on looking after anyone who needed looking after, which amounted to nearly all the Moores — Grandmother, Uncle George, Aunt Lucy, and elderly cousins that everyone else had forgotten. He was a man naturally inclined toward benevolence, but can't such an inclination become a burden too?

"Miss Kate would leave when she pleased," Fergus reminded me. "Don't forget her hay fever."

Grandmother's hay fever dictated a trip every fall. She got on a train and left the state for some other where ragweed wasn't pollinating. Her family had scattered by then. She visited a sister in Pennsylvania, the brother in the Texas Panhandle. More often she went to a spa like Saratoga or Red Boiling Springs. And she travelled alone. A few years after Grandpa died she announced she'd cured herself of hay fever by eating the local honey.

Fergus' comment was, "She would have had to have eaten

about fifty gallons of it. Miss Kate lost her reason for going. She didn't have to get away from the farm anymore."

"But she usually spoke of Grandpa as if she adored him."

"Sure. Sure she did. They admired each other. He did everything she wouldn't have dared to do and she . . . she was such a model of respectable behavior he couldn't help but admire her."

"You keep throwing the old opposites theory at me." Fergus took a long puff on his cigar. He often used it to underline his opinions in the same way that pipe smokers point the stems of their pipes or make people wait while they puff and consider an importunate question.

"Honey, I can't come up with nothing no better."

This was another of Fergus' tricks, to switch to bad English when he wanted to make a point. In the country music business to be able to talk "country" was a necessity. It was also an effective way of disparaging someone else's opinion. By playing the ignoramus, he could at the same time play the sage, plainspoken hick. At times like this I thought I saw Grandpa's influence coming through again, or maybe it was just the cigar that made me think of him and tobacco.

Aunt Lucy floated back in just as I spoke of seeing tobacco in his fields.

"Now, you have that wrong. Papa only raised tobacco once. He said it was too much worry."

"It wasn't just worry about the crop," Uncle Phillip interrupted. "He said it was too hard on his barn. Curing, the way he did it, required a hardwood fire burning slow on the floor of the barn and lasted nearly three weeks. You never saw that done did you, Marianne?"

I hadn't. I knew almost nothing about the real business of farming. Grandpa's only son Uncle George didn't like what he knew. He was far more interested in buying and selling land than he was in plowing and harvesting, so in 1941, four years after Grandpa died, Uncle George sold the farm, moved into

town with Miss Kate, and took up auctioneering first, then
real estate. I wondered briefly what Grandpa would have
thought about that.

"Well, he was a trader himself," said Fergus.

"Papa wasn't sentimental about farming. He liked the look
of the land, the way certain fields lay, and he took pride in
what he could raise but he always planned for us to leave the
place — all of us. He insisted on college educations, girls
included. Papa was a great believer in education." Aunt Lucy
got up again and went to the dining room.

"I want to show you something. You haven't seen it in
years." She held up a wax apple with teeth marks on it.

For an instant I was seven years old again tasting wax instead of the tart apple I'd expected, and Fergus was laughing
just as he laughed then. Of course he was the one who had
dared me to take the fruit from Grandmother's cut-glass bowl
on her dining table. Of course I chose the apple; I liked it best.
It was a strong primary red, darker on one side than the other.

"Did you keep the rest of it, Aunt Lucy?" Once there was
a bunch of grapes, a banana, a pear, two plums, two peaches,
and an orange. All were wax, all beautifully colored and
shaded to ripe perfection, or so they appeared to me in those
pre-plastic days. By some childish twist of logic I had not
thought to wonder why the fruit never spoiled. Perhaps I
unconsciously assumed everything in my grandmother's house
stayed quietly perfect in the way old people seem always the
same age to children.

"That kind of thing went out of style, and Mother put them
in the attic. One hot summer they must have collapsed. Only
the apple kept its shape. When we cleared out the house I
threw the rest away."

The truth is sometimes a poor, sad thing — wax fruit
melted in an attic, a lone mule wandering on the front lawn,
a mute player piano — a few insubstantial fragments. All we
could do was grab hold and make something more of them. I
turned the apple in my hands.

"It's a grief, clearing out a house after someone's gone. But you can't keep everything. You'd never believe that though looking at Fergus' office."

"The ghost of Miss Kate flies through there on white angel wings around four every morning. Sometimes people hear her screaming." Fergus grinned.

"And Grandpa's ghost?"

"Oh, his is still riding through the Arcade on a mule." The Arcade is a short covered passageway through the middle of a block in downtown Nashville. Small stores used to face pedestrians on either side. I don't know what's there now or if it's even still used.

"Why did he do that?"

"He'd been up to Nashville to see some friends," Fergus said and looked at the ceiling as if he wished I hadn't asked.

"You mean he'd been up all night drinking," Aunt Lucy intervened. "I know he did that kind of thing. I swear, the way he treats me, you'd think I was Mother. She'd hardly let anybody say 'whiskey' in front of her."

"Yes," Fergus went on, "Well . . . he rode through the Arcade and found a policeman waiting for him on the other side. And the policeman said, 'I'm fining you five dollars for disorderly conduct.'

"Grandpa pulled some money out of his pocket, 'Here's ten dollars. I'm going back the same way.' He turned the mule around and rode through again, went on back to the farm I reckon."

I saw him with the sun rising over the stubby green hills, a portly squire, his jacket rumpled, his face reddened, his watch chain strained against his belly. He was a little sleepy. He let the mule settle into a slow walk, then shook himself awake and trotted off into the countryside through the perpetual mist that surrounds mythical figures.

Afterword

"FINE STORIES. They delight and instruct," my fictional Gramp Tom Northway would have said. "They show the truth in human relationships," I can hear my Grandmother Florence say. "They're funny too," says Grandma Nellie, "and sad." "And wise," my Grandpa Frank, the judge, would say.

That, I think, would be the response of my own "Grands" to these stories, as it is mine.

For a number of years I have considered Carolyn Osborn one of Texas' most distinctive framers of short fiction, and the most original voice among Texas writers. Her stories are structured and harmonized by Carolyn's sense of life. They have integrity, never departing from Carolyn's sense of life as she conceives it in her narratives. With Osborn this amounts to a kind of life-adaptive, fresh narrative form that subordinates, but does not abandon the traditional method of resolving conflict in artificially plotted fiction. (If you think about it, it is this same integrity of conception from philosophy through form that makes us respect and enjoy the work of such distinctive writers as Joyce, Mansfield, Hemingway and Welty.)

For Osborn life is conflicting relationships, their endless mysteries, and the resignation of the human being caught up in the psychological and practical network of life. Each is a contained "system," self-woven, attached, often inexplicably, to other human "systems." Her "plot" is her own distinctive form, but addresses the oldest kind of human question in fiction: "Why does A love B who loves C?"

For me it makes true, refreshing and valuable fiction in human terms.

In these stories, as in her first two collections, we find the quirkiness of character, wry humor and Osbornian turn of phrase that propel the stories, making "Cowboy Movie" a small masterpiece and "Greats" and "Grands" memorable. In theme, they are stories of resignation — a kind of stoicism not far from Hemingway's — that deal with the adversarial relationship between women and men. All the characters in all the stories are "Warriors and Maidens." The precise depiction of female consciousness that dominates the stories makes the writer's insight into the male protagonist in the fulcrum story "The Warrior and the Maiden" even more remarkably effective. A world of contemporary consciousness, with strong roots in the past has been created here, and it stays true to itself story by story, line by line.

They are good stuff because Carolyn Osborn has lived and experienced joy and tragedy and knows what she is writing about. She knows about her characters, has observed them from their toenails to their sandals. She knows her settings — ranch or Santa Fe or Paris or Austin or suburban street. She knows how things work, or don't, so there is a fine sense of verisimilitude of place, of putting together and taking apart, and things. Good fiction should forever be chock-full of things, treats of the senses, correlatives to the meaning, of mules, flowers, trash, whiskey, old cars, rocks, shadows, water, sunsets, funny hats. . . . *Vide* "The Gardener" for an example of a whole fiction and its psychology organized around this principle.

Then, for me, there is the strength of this writer's sense of time. I feel at home with her as I attempt in my own Northway stories this same kind of fiction: a netting back and drawing forth, as in "Greats" and "Grands," from the waters of time whatever can be retrieved of value. These values bond for us the present with the individual human past. Through all the stories in *Warriors and Maidens* is the sense of "time past and time present" and our own little, finite consciousness. And that makes her often seemingly humorous stories serious.

Enough said. Fiction and poetry remain, after all, the last realms of writer speaking to reader individually. So each of us may relish now going back and reading these fine stories once again.

— Marshall Terry
Southern Methodist University